# You, me and Destiny

## J.F. Mc Loughlin

Chapter 1

My life hung by a thread. Desperate thoughts raced through my mind. I was feeling faint but strove to remain alert. I took a deep breath.

My chest ached.

'Danny, stay with us! Please stay with us'.

There was urgency in the paramedic's tone.

One lapse into unconsciousness and it could be curtains for me.

I was not ready to die, not now when there was so much to attend to.

Tears of frustration welled up in my eyes. I was determined to remain strong. There was blood everywhere. It was all my blood. The lorry had smashed into the passenger side of my car. After the airbag activated, an explosion of dust had filled the inside of the vehicle. My throat was irritated. I desperately needed a drink. I thought I was getting sick but it was blood, which was spewing out of me. I tried to occupy my mind by piecing together what had happened.

I reckoned that the collision had been my fault. My mind had not been on the road. I couldn't even remember seeing the traffic light. All I know is that I did not stop, not until after the collision anyway.

I could hear the sound of cutting equipment. The rescue crew was attempting to free me from the wreckage. Words of encouragement were coming to me from outside the car. Despite my best efforts, I was beginning to drift off. My breathing was becoming increasingly laboured as if my windpipe was obstructed.

A sudden chill swept over my entire body.

I could feel cold beads of perspiration on my forehead and around my eyes. I tried to use my hand to wipe them away. My hand did not respond. I didn't know whether it was trapped or paralysed. Without warning, my body experienced a series of involuntary convulsions. I soon realised that I had lost control of my broken body. I tried to shout but I was unable to.

I must have passed out. When I regained consciousness, I was free of the wreckage and appeared to be at some remove from the vehicle. What I was viewing made no sense to me. I was observing the scene from some distance, as if through the wrong end of a pair of binoculars. I was looking down at the rescue workers as they dealt with the wreckage. Inexplicably, they seemed to be attending another victim, who also appeared to have been trapped in my car. How could that be? I had been travelling alone.

In a moment, almost as if someone had turned around the binoculars, I got a close-up view of the casualty.

It was like looking in the mirror.

I realised that I was hovering above my own body.

Whatever blood I still had in my veins ran cold. I was petrified, desperately hoping that this disembodiment was temporary.

For what seemed an eternity, was probably no more than a few moments, I continued to hover above the scene. A small crowd had gathered to observe. There was no conversation. They just looked on in eerie silence. I could see one lady make the sign of the cross. A passing priest stopped to pray over my body as it was placed on the stretcher. I tried to communicate with him. He leaned in closer. Judging from his blank expression, I don't think he understood me. I just wanted him to tell my nearest and dearest that I loved them, just in case I didn't make it.

The ambulance doors closed. In a moment, with blue lights flashing and sirens blaring, it was on its way to the hospital. The awful thing was that it had left without me.

Chapter 2

I was at a marketing conference with my boss, Andrew when the news came to me. The word was that he was in a critical condition. My head was in a tizzy. Andrew drove me to the hospital. He sped through many amber and some reddening lights I did not want him to rush. If the news was good, time was not of the essence. If the news was bad, then ignorance was certainly bliss for me. Something inside of me told me to be prepared for the worst. I asked Andrew to slow down.

Danny and I had been together for nearly seven years and married for five of those years. He was the love of my life. I know that some viewed him as an opinionated git but he was my opinionated git and I was mad about him. He was without doubt, the most important person in my life and I'm sure that he felt similarly about me. He was still in his thirties and I had confidently hoped that we would partner each other into ripe old age. I didn't want to lose him now.

Not knowing whether he would be alive or dead when I reached the hospital played havoc with my mind. Conflicting thoughts competed for influence. I prayed that he would not be taken unless the alternative was his existing only in a vegetative state. I knew that if Danny were to be given a choice, he would opt for death over total incapacity any day. As the car drew closer to the hospital, I struggled to contain my emotions. I could feel my heart racing. My stomach was churning, as wave after wave of nausea continued to sweep over me. For one awful moment, I feared I might throw up in my boss's new *BMW*. I needed to distract myself from nausea. I attempted to focus on prayer.

I had not been to church in years and praying was a rare activity for me. However, in the twenty-minute journey, I prayed with fervour, which was hitherto unknown to me. I promised God that if he left Danny to me, that I would be a reformed character. I would attend church every week, recite daily prayers and live an exemplary life. Being left without my Danny would be Hell on earth. I needed him to live. As I entered the hospital, the heart-chilling thought crossed my mind that I might already be a widow.

Despite his reputation for being something of a cold fish, Andrew was being very supportive. He wrapped his arm around me as he guided me along the passageway to the *Emergency Department*. Alongside us, some clerical staff and medics went about their everyday business. The hospital was their performance space and we were just extras, who were in for the day.

Out of the corner of my eye, I caught sight of a young mother and her new baby on their way home after a joyous birth. A proud dad followed in their wake, carrying his partner's overnight case and some celebratory balloons.

I had wanted a baby. Danny was lukewarm on the subject, insisting that there was no rush. I knew that, should he survive this, we would attempt to start a family. Time was moving on. I wanted a baby and hoped that there would not be a problem with conception.

Andrew brought me back from my reveries, by directing me through the double-doors of the *Emergency Department.*

Andrew made some enquiries. His tone was urgent and demanding.

He sought someone to aid us.

A passing nurse sensed his agitation and approached him.

'This lady here is Lucy Keane. Her husband, Danny was brought in here after a very serious road accident. Is there any update on his condition?'

Her face betrayed the gravity of the situation.

She was obviously au-fait with his case.

'Mrs Keane, I'm afraid your husband is critical. He is in theatre right now undergoing emergency surgery, and he is likely to be there for some considerable time.'

It was difficult to know whether to be relieved or disappointed.

On the positive side, he was still alive. Highly competent surgeons were doing their very best for him. However, he was critical and there were no words of encouragement coming my way.

'Do you think he will make it?' I blurted out, knowing full well that this was a question, which could not be answered.

'As I said, your husband is critical. The doctors are attempting to stabilise his condition. He has lost a lot of blood and he is suffering from multiple injuries.'

'Such as?' Andrew enquired.

She was not to be drawn.

'I think you should wait for the surgeon'.

It was evident that we were in a real life and death battle.

The nurse had other duties to attend to. She understood my concern and pointed to some chairs opposite.

'I'm sorry that I cannot be more helpful or encouraging but I can assure you that the surgery team will do everything in its power to save your husband. My advice is that you should get a cup of tea and as soon as there is anything to report, I will arrange for the surgeon to come down to speak to you'.

It was not supposed to be like this. With it being Valentine's Day, we had plans for a romantic meal that night. That meal was now on hold, as indeed was the rest of my life.

My Danny was somewhere upstairs in the operating theatre. He was fighting for his life. There was absolutely nothing that I could do to assist him. I felt so helpless. At least he was not suffering now and was beyond all worry and stress. I nearly envied him in his unconscious state.

I felt sorry for Andrew. He had drawn the short straw. Even though we worked together, we had little personal dealings. I knew precious little about the man and he knew as little about me. The total of my knowledge was that he and his wife had divorced some years ago and that it had been a childless union. In the office, he had the reputation of being a workaholic.

'Well, Lucy, it's still all to play for', he said encouragingly.

I nodded. 'At least he's still with us,' I answered, showing my crossed fingers to him.

'God is good', he added soothingly but unconvincingly.

I tried to be strong and optimistic but was failing miserably on both counts. I suddenly felt overwhelmed by feelings of helplessness and despair. In seconds, I was reduced to being a pathetic, blubbering fool. Andrew looked around for some inspiration or assistance. Disappointed in both, he opened up his arms to give me a comforting embrace. My world was crumbling before my eyes. Tragedy had cruelly stripped me bare, both emotionally and physically.

Some moments later, the hospital chaplain arrived on the scene. He had surely played a supporting role in similar dramas. Andrew took advantage of his arrival to go and take care of some business. I was glad. Having to converse with him just added to my discomfort.

The chaplain was an avuncular figure, with empathy etched across his timeworn face. He took my hand tenderly in his. At least I had the advantage of having a man of God in my corner. It might do no good but it was worth a try.
He had clearly been briefed on the details of the accident.
'I can only imagine how anxious you must feel now. I want you to know that I am here for you now and for Danny also when he recovers consciousness.'
These words of optimism provided me at least with a straw to clutch at. I thanked him for his support
'Not at all, my dear! Life throws some curveballs at us all. At a time like this, you should always remember that you are never alone. My dear, God loves us unconditionally. However, His ways are not our ways and we can't always understand them', he offered, by way of explanation.
That did little to reassure me.
        The priest invited me to pray with him. I readily agreed. At that moment I would have considered praying to the devil if it held out any prospect of a happy ending.
'Yes Father, I would like that'.
With his earnest eyes firmly closed, he prayed with conviction, interceding with the Almighty on my Danny's behalf. In my book, that could never be a bad thing. He finished his intercession with 'Pray for us sinners, now and at the hour of our death'. With that, he placed a comforting hand on my shoulder. 'Amen', I sighed.

Chapter 3

I was still a spectator on my life, perhaps on my death also. It was mind-blowing. I was hovering somehow above the operating theatre. Below me, I could see the gowned medics frantically working on my anesthetised body. From the snatches of conversation that I caught, it was clear that my condition posed enormous challenges.

Lucy, whom I had seen during my disembodied wanderings, was downstairs, totally traumatised. A smartly dressed man supported her. I presumed that he was a colleague, who had driven her to the hospital. She had frequently spoken of several of these work colleagues. I was never really listening to her, yet I had become familiar with certain names. This one might be David or Andrew or Arthur. I hadn't met any of them. I never wanted to meet them either. I figured that most of those involved in marketing belonged to a world, which I had little tolerance of. They were piggybacking on entrepreneurs, who were risk-takers and productive. My area was in software development where practical services and solutions were delivered in the marketplace. We made something tangible and critical to the efficiency of production.

For all that, I couldn't know if all of that activity was now behind me.

I seemed to be locked into a half-world of sorts. It was certainly one in which I was utterly inept and powerless. Everything seemed transient and fluid. One moment, I was watching Lucy, crying her eyes out on a hospital bench and the next moment I was viewing my own body from above. It was mind-blowing.

Just as a television director selects the particular camera-shot, he wishes to use, I sensed that a controller was calling the shots in my surreal world. It was unnerving and frustrating. I was like a frightened little boy, lost in a strange and terrifying world. This little boy could not call for help. He could neither be seen nor heard. It needed to end and end soon. I wanted to escape from this lifeless limbo and its torment. I seemed to be all mind and no body, or viewed from the operating theatre, all body and no mind. I was no longer whole. I was just a fragmented version of my old self, which I needed to defragment.

I wanted to run downstairs to my dearest Lucy, hug her tightly and assure her that all would be fine but I couldn't. What if it wasn't all going to be fine? Suppose these were some of my final moments in this mortal world. If that were the case, then I would leave this world a broken man, both physically and mentally. I would feel cheated. I would be blaming myself for all eternity. I would hate myself for not giving Lucy the child she had craved and I would hate myself for not being there for little Alfie when he needed me.

I sensed that control of my life had passed from my hands. Whoever was in charge now had directed me to the small, hospital oratory. Maybe that person was suggesting that it was time to say my prayers but I just couldn't pray. I just could not focus for a sufficient length of time, to marshal my thoughts and aspirations. I wondered if there was the point in having me there at all.

By now, I felt sure, that there was nothing random about my re-positioning. I felt sure that this entire drama was being coordinated. The director of this nightmare had a very particular purpose in mind.

Soon, I understood that I was there to get another glimpse at Lucy. I sincerely hoped that it would not be the last. I observed

Lucy arrive. She looked forlorn. She stood for a moment before the small table, which served as an altar before tearfully taking a pew. I observed two others arrive shortly afterwards. Both seemed absorbed in their respective anguish. My thoughts were not with them. My heart broke for Lucy. She was never particularly religious no more than I was but we both prayed in desperate situations.

I stared at Lucy as she sat there. After a few moments, I observed her reach into her pocket to grab her mobile phone. I watched her power it up before dragging the side button to mute.

I could read that she had five or six missed calls, as well as a series of unread text messages. She scrolled her way through these, without reading any. Lucy then swiped back the screen to display her list of favourites. My name was first on that list. She selected my name and began to compose a new message. On the virtual keyboard, she wrote:

'Danny, my sweet Valentine, I will love you forever. Get well soon'.

She pressed the *SEND* option but not before she added her trademark smiley face.

How I wished that I could respond to her text!

There was so much I wanted to say to her. Apart from communicating my undying love, I wanted to exhort her to be strong. It would be a different Valentine's Day for both of us. Perhaps this time next year, we might be looking back on this as being the darkest period in our lives.

If I were lucky enough to be given a reprieve, I would be a different man. My priority would be to start a family. I had been quickly educated to appreciate that a baby is the greatest gift and I am sorry that I denied Lucy that gift, a gift that she had so craved. I had been such a fool.

The director overseeing this production was preparing for my next scene. I was moving again or at least I was experiencing the sensation of movement. Maybe my surroundings were moving. I could no longer be certain about anything. I was leaving the hospital behind. I had no clue where I was going. It was not so much a case of being sucked into a vortex than being eased onto something much gentler, like a fairground carousel. Curiously, the movement did not appear to have forward momentum. If anything I felt that I was being transported in a backward motion.

I now had that a feeling that I had company. I sensed that the presence was benign. Then, amazingly, I had a feeling that my brain was being in some way, adjusted or fine-tuned. It was as if there was a process of deletion and insertion taking place on my brain's motherboard. Intuitively, I felt that time would be unwound in some inexplicable way. I wondered if my recent memories were in danger of being deleted. Like a disk being formatted on a computer, my mind might well have some, or all of its memory erased.

As my journey continued, I could see a bewildering array of fast-moving pictures or excerpts from my previous life, flash past, like an old-style slide show. They appeared and disappeared with such rapidity that I could not focus on any of them. As with rewinding a video it quickly became tiresome on the eyes. I felt myself grow increasingly tired and listless. I was being put into a sort of hibernation. As with a laptop computer, I was being shut down to be re-started.

Chapter 4

Three hours had passed and I was still waiting for an update on Danny. My sixth sense suggested that he was slipping away from me. When this fear began to take root in my mind, I sent an emergency text to my best friend, Karen Doyle. I knew that when Karen received my text, she would drop whatever she had been doing, to join me. I could rely on her. In this time of trouble, she was the one person I could call on.

When she arrived, she hugged me tightly and sought to reassure me. The more I cried, the tighter she hugged me. I filled her in on the horrific details. She was worried but was determined to be strong for me. She had dispelled the tears, which had been welling up in her eyes and replaced them with a steely resolve.

Karen located the coffee machine and returned holding two steaming cups of strong brew. One cup was thrust into my trembling hand.

'Get that down, girl,' she insisted.

I didn't feel much like drinking it. Karen was in mammy mode and was difficult to resist. When I checked my mobile phone, she must have thought that I was being bothered by work-related calls.

' No, I was just looking at the last text, I sent to Danny'.

I invited her to read it.

The poignancy of the content stymied her best attempts at being the calm super-heroine for me. I could see that a stubborn tear was already forming in her eye. Even the steely Karen, could not suppress her sensitive and empathetic nature.

' That was so sweet, Lucy, so sweet. I just hope that it won't be your final text to him'.

I certainly hoped so.

Karen was back to her reassuring best.

'Danny will put up a good fight anyway. Let's face it, he doesn't know any other way'.

'True, Karen! He is a scrapper, isn't he?'

'He sure is'.

When I returned from a trip to the toilets, Karen was off again, in search of something or other. I was glad of these few moments to be alone with my thoughts. Karen probably needed a moment to herself too.

She had earlier pressed me to eat something. I had no appetite. How could I think of food at a time like this?

Karen was having none of it. She felt that I needed to have food in my stomach, to be strong, for whatever I might have to deal with. From the canteen, she brought a salad sandwich and a still-steaming bowl of vegetable soup, together with two slices of bread.

'It will keep the wind out of your stomach', she declared. 'You will need to keep your strength up, if only for Danny's sake.'

'You will make someone a great mother one day'. I teased her.

'And so will you, she smiled'.

I certainly hoped so but things were not looking great.

Karen was always in my corner and I always respected her opinions, except when it came to her early reservations about Danny. She had not warmed to him at all. In truth, even I had reservations about him in those early days.

Danny Keane was an acquired taste and the more I got to know him, the more I loved him. First impressions can be misleading. He was very set in his views, showing nothing but contempt for contrary opinions. Underneath that abrasive and intolerant exterior, I soon discovered that Danny was as insecure as the rest of us.

A double -whammy had turned his young world upside down, when his parents died tragically from carbon monoxide poisoning. It was one of those tragedies one reads about in the papers and quickly forgets. Danny could never forget. He had learned to live with the loss of the only family he had but he could never forget. I closed my eyes and said a quick prayer that tragedy would not engulf the last surviving Keane.

I froze when I saw a tall man in surgical garb approach. 'Jesus, Mary and Joseph help me now!' I feared the worst.
I was too nervous to breathe.
To my traumatised eyes, his movements seemed almost to be in slow motion. I tried to read his expression. His face was inscrutable. I stood up to hear my fate. Karen stood alongside me, taking a firm grip of my left arm. My legs felt wobbly. I should have remained sitting.
Time seemed to stand still. It seemed an age before he opened his down-turned mouth.
His words were uttered slowly and falteringly. However, the content was clear and stark.
'I'm so very sorry, Mrs Keane. Your husband didn't make it.'
Those five words shattered my world.

Being hit by an articulated truck could not have been more devastating. My breathing hurt. My heart ached and my knees buckled under me. I slumped back down into the chair. The room seemed to go into a spin and the voice of the doctor waned and became more and more distant until it seemed little more than an echo. I was feeling nauseous but tried hard to overcome the sensation.
The surgeon continued to speak. I had zoned out. It was as if he were talking to someone else. I tuned in again as he explained what happened.

'Saving him was always going to be an uphill battle. Early on, we seemed to be winning. Suddenly, he went into cardiac arrest. We tried our best to resuscitate him. It was to no avail. Our best efforts seemed impotent, it was as if he were being pulled or dragged away from us.'

The words cut me to the quick.

He had a question for me.

'If I may mention something, which might be viewed as insensitive, at this terrible moment, yet is of critical importance. I am referring to organ donation.'

Danny, for many years, had carried an organ donor card.

'Mrs Keane, your husband's heart, lungs and kidneys were compromised to such an extent, that they were rendered incapable of being transplanted but if you permit us, his eyes could be of benefit to others.'

I hated the idea of his body parts being, in some way pilfered, yet I was not going to go against his wishes.

I nodded my consent.

I zoned out again and heard no more. A thousand thoughts were running through my head, mostly selfish thoughts about how I would cope without him in my life. I was conscious of Karen, exchanging some words with the surgeon, but I had no idea what she had been saying. I was in a world of my own looking at this drama unfold before my eyes. It is very difficult to describe one's feelings in such a situation. I felt that I had been savagely mugged and my husband snatched from me.

After what seemed an eternity, we were ushered into the family room, by a very considerate nursing sister, who sat us down and spoke tenderly to me. She told me that a doctor was on his way to advise me on medication to help me cope with what was unfolding.

Andrew, my manager had not gone very far. Most likely he had escaped to his car to make some phone calls, probably acquainting colleagues with developments. He had now returned to my side. He did not have to ask what had transpired. He didn't need to. He just embraced me, supported my head in his arms. I could feel his face against mine and I could feel his tears mingle with mine. I needed to be held and I was glad that he was there to support me.

The elderly chaplain reappeared. He also embraced me and exhorted me to be strong. He told me that he had given Danny the Last Rites when he was admitted. He had not mentioned it earlier, fearing that I might be needlessly alarmed.

'Danny is in a better place', he said, in a vain attempt to be comforting. 'And I feel sure that he will be looking down on you and assisting you in every way. God, my dear, will give you the strength to bear the cross He has given you'.

To me, this response was little more than polite, meaningless words. It brought me no comfort. In fact, there were no words in the dictionary, which could have brought me any comfort. I was desolate. I was alone. My world had been shattered. The love of my life had been taken away from me. I would never see Danny again, never hear his voice and never feel his strong arms around me. He had his life in front of him and now he was gone at just thirty -eight years of age. February 14 would be the day that my world stopped turning.

Chapter 5

I was not fully conscious. Despite this, I was somehow aware of things or at least, I was absorbing information. The sensation of being transported continued for me. Like a kid sleeping in the back seat of the family car, I was sick and tired, yet wondering if we were there yet.

Apart from utter bewilderment regarding my predicament, my thoughts were with Lucy. She must be going through hell, as she waited around that hospital, while I drifted somewhere or nowhere in a state of limbo, travelling between life and death. I hoped that when this particular journey or escapade ended, that I would be reunited with her. Lucy and I were a team. I was no good without her and I liked to think that she would be better with me alongside her. Together we could lay the foundations for a happy family.

My unstable mental state was playing tricks on me. I didn't know whether I was hallucinating or whether I had an actual visitation. A disembodied face suddenly appeared to me. It was a spherical, luminous face, somewhat akin to how the man in the moon was depicted in nursery rhymes. This visage had a kindly aspect. As the image crystallised, I recognised a familiar face from my childhood.

It was that of a long-deceased, older man from my childhood days in Dromahair. Tommie had been a close friend of my dad. He had worked his smallholding, which was located less than a mile down the road from our home. Throughout my childhood, Tommie was a very popular visitor to our home. I particularly liked his chatty and amusing ways. He had a fund of stories from ancient Ireland, with tales of the fairies and the paranormal. He would also regale me with chilling tales of wandering spirits, doomed to walk the earth for a set time because of certain errors or omissions in their earthy lives.

I waited for him to speak and when he did, it was in the same soft tones as he had done in the past. Hearing him again produced a momentary warm nostalgic feeling.

'Hi Danny, long time no see. I didn't expect to see you so soon though', he remarked as casually as if we had just met at the crossroads.

I had not planned on seeing him either. I was so distracted that I didn't know whether I replied or not.

He seemed to sense my disorientation and bewilderment.

'Danny, I don't have long now. This is just a flying visit to look in on you. I will be back to chat to you when we know where you are heading. I'll tell you one thing though, we need to clear that head of yours.'

I wasn't sure what he meant but I was glad that, at least, I still seemed to have a head.

I wondered how much he was able to read my thoughts and preoccupations. I detected a definite note of concern or admonishment in his tone.

'You can't go anywhere, with all that stuff going on in your head. You have to clear it out first, as you would dung out of a stable. My job is to help you get the show back on the road.'

I could certainly do with some sort of explanation of what was going on but the bottom line was that I could not be sure, whether this was a dream or a visitation from my old neighbour. I lacked the presence of mind to ask.

'Before I go, I have something for you to see'.

He disappeared as suddenly and as inexplicably, as he had appeared.

In a moment or so I was shown the harrowing scene of a distraught Lucy being assisted out of the hospital by her good friend Karen. I was also shown a white-coated medic signing a series of official-looking documents, as my body lay on a hospital bed. Finally, I watched, as my body was taken out of the hospital ward, into what appeared to be an outside building, presumably a morgue. I couldn't say whether I was dead or just going mad. Neither scenario was in any way, appealing. What, if anything, did the future hold for me if indeed I had a future?

Chapter 6

I understood. Other patients needed the room. We had spent an hour with Danny's remains in a sideward and now, we were being politely requested to vacate the room.

They were ready to transfer Danny to the morgue. He was no longer a living, breathing person. He was now just the lifeless remains of one. As the carcass of a chicken might be thoughtlessly tossed into the bin after Sunday lunch, my Danny was being unceremoniously removed to a morgue.

Karen never left my side. Without her, it would have been impossible for me to cope. I was so overwhelmed that I could not even think straight. I knew that I ought to be contacting people and making funeral arrangements but I was stupefied by this unfolding tragedy. Thankfully Karen was there for me.

Using my mobile phone, she broke the news to my sister Kate in London and to my brother Mark in Sligo. I hated causing them upset or distress and I could only imagine their shock. We are a close family. They would be shattered to hear of Danny's death but they would be sadder still, for what that meant for me. Mark and Danny had always got on well. They were quite similar, both being no-nonsense alpha males.

I knew that my sister would be on the first available flight. Her husband, Trevor, was a decent, hard-working Englishman. They had two beautiful young daughters. Kate was two years my senior. Despite this relative proximity in age, she was always mature beyond her years. She taught me a host of girlie skills, like how to apply makeup and make the most of my natural assets. Most importantly, she helped me project confidence, even when I didn't have much. Head held high over the shoulders, eyes forward and a fixed smile on my face were all elements that helped create the public me.

Karen had contacted the local undertaker. He needed a quick word with me, as I had to authorise them to collect the remains and take care of arrangements.

He was used to dealing with the bereaved and well understood that I was in shock. He kept it simple and assured me that he would take care of everything. When he mentioned that he would ring my parish priest to arrange the church services, it drove home the harsh reality of the situation. It was surreal. Uunfortunately, it was fast becoming so very real. My husband's funeral was being arranged. Short of seeing him in a coffin, how more final could it be?

I mentioned this to Karen. There was no way that this could possibly be sugar-coated or played down.

'There is no point in telling you otherwise. It's going to be a living nightmare for you. However, I now you will have all the support that we can give you. You will not have to face it alone'.

That was all very well but even if I were surrounded by hundreds of people, I would still be facing it alone. That was the terrible future, which awaited me.

Karen was being practical. Someone had to be. As the day wore on, she acted as a go-between for me until my family arrived. There were many decisions to be made. Poor Karen was anticipating upcoming events and heading off any likely problems. She was trying to do my thinking for me.

I was reluctant to consider anything about his funeral service. In my state of denial, I hoped the entire tragedy would just go away if I chose to ignore it. I wanted no funeral. I wanted him with me, forever. That clearly was not going to happen and some decisions had to be made.

'Did Danny ever talk to you about his wishes or did he ever express an opinion either way on cremation or burial?' Karen asked.

I looked at her in disbelief. What healthy man in his thirties plans his funeral?

We never had such morbid conversations, no more than we had discussions about his choice of destination when he would have qualified for the free travel scheme.

However, I had that decision to make and I had to make it soon. I knew it would make no difference to Danny at this stage but it would make a difference to me. I shared my unformed thoughts with Karen. Burial was particularly harsh and primitive. How more cruel can it get than to have a widow stand there, watching her loved one being planted in the soil, like the remains of a dumb animal. On the other hand, there would always be a grave, a permanent focal point for me. Then again, graveyards were always associated in my mind with bleakness, with cold winds and with spookiness.

But was cremation any better?

When all was said and done, it was burning him in a fire like a giant sod of turf.

On the other hand, I could have Danny's remains with me always, possibly in an urn on my mantelpiece. Maybe it might give me a sense of his presence. Part of him would still be with me but would it not be a constant reminder of my enormous loss? Karen was still considering various scenarios, hoping that one of them might be a little less palatable than the others for me.

'Instead of keeping the ashes in an urn, you could scatter them somewhere that was very special to him, such as a location, which might be associated with good memories or with happy times'.

That was very true. I had often heard of families of sea-faring folk, having the remains of their loved ones scattered at sea and of course newspaper reports of the odd football fanatic, wishing to have his remains scattered in the centre circle of his team's home ground. Danny wasn't like that. The only place he ever spoke of, which I associated with fond memories for him, was his childhood home. He loved roaming the fields there and just sitting on a big rock, in one particular field there. He used to love being alone there, just thinking or figuring out life, as it was being unfolded to him.

That thought gave me a certain little bit of comfort. Perhaps this was the way to go? But Danny had sold that land some years previously to a local farmer. I felt sure that this neighbour would have no objection to my scattering Danny's ashes on the ground there, should I decide to take the cremation option.

Unlike Karen, I had never been to a cremation service. She talked me through the procedure. After a religious ceremony, the coffin was placed on a glorified conveyor belt and brought behind some obscuring curtains. This sounded more appropriate, less chilling than burial. It seemed apt, like a final curtain call for one's life here and the commencement of a journey to, what was hopefully another life.

My decision had been made. Danny's remains would be cremated and at a later stage, his remains would be scattered on the fields, which acted as the backdrop for his childhood years.

Chapter 7

I no longer had any concept of time or how it was passing. I was still moving but at a rather gentle pace. I was eerily alone with my thoughts for what seemed an eternity. It is amazing that a very short while ago, I did not even know of Alfie's existence and now he had been exalted to the level, which hitherto, my wife of five years, had solely occupied.

Ten years earlier, three years before I first met Lucy, I used to frequent a little coffee shop, near my workplace in Dublin. It was owned and operated by a cheery and pleasant girl called Suzi. She had qualified as an architect but was just indulging her passion for food. Suzi had a bright and breezy personality. She was so easy to like. Over the months, I got closer to the chic blonde. Pretty soon we began to date.

It wasn't serious for either of us, a no-strings-attached, fun-filled arrangement. We enjoyed each other's company on two or three occasions a week. That might have been for a drink, a film or the occasional meal. We had good fun. Soon a physical intimacy developed between us. While it had been exciting, it was rather short-lived. We just grew apart.

There was no rancour, no bitterness, and no emotional scars, not on my part anyway. We just went our separate ways. I moved offices and found myself a new coffee shop and I presumed that she had moved on with her life too.

Nowadays, people can stalk or track ex-partners on social media platforms. Back then a clean break seemed possible. I did not see sign or sight of her or even hear of her after that. That was not until the morning of the accident, February 14.

At about ten o'clock that morning, I took a call at my desk. Despite the passage of time, I instantly recognised Suzi's voice. Hearing her again brought a smile to my face. I had nothing good memories of her. On this occasion, she sounded unusually serious, not at all like the old Suzi, whom I had known and loved. She told me that she was in a difficult situation and she wanted to ask me for a big favour. She made a point of explaining that she was not looking for money. Even if she were, I would not have had any hesitation in obliging her. She wanted to see me urgently and she warned me to brace myself for a bit of a shock. I made some arrangements for an extended lunch break and agreed to meet her in a hotel on the Naas Road as it had easy access for both of us.

As soon as our eyes met we both smiled. I stood up and gave her a tight hug. While I was embracing her, I could feel that she was trembling and upset. I released her from my embrace and held her at arm's length to survey the changes. She was as young and as pretty looking as ever but those bright eyes were reddening from salty tears.

'Hey! What's wrong?' I asked.

Before she could answer, a waitress arrived to take our order.Suzi did not seem interested. I ordered soup and sandwiches.

'Better get something inside you', I said, beginning to sound a bit of a mammy.

She then took out her mobile phone from her pocket and thumbed through some pictures, before settling on one particular photo. She handed me the phone to view the photo.

It was a picture of a good looking, young boy of nine or ten, not much dissimilar from myself at that age. It could have been my Confirmation picture, as it was quite similar to one of me, which my mother had kept for years on the mantelpiece, back home in Dromahair.

'It's like a photo of me as a youngster!'

She smiled.

'Yes, he is incredibly like you. Then again why wouldn't he be?'

The penny dropped very quickly.

My face must have registered my absolute shock.

She grabbed hold of my hand and looked me straight in the eye.

'I know this is an awful shock for you, Danny but this here is your son. Alfie is his name.'

I was dumbfounded.

I just sat there, like a pig in a stupor.

She gave a moment for it to register.

You could have knocked me down with a feather.

'How? How can this be? I stuttered, more by way of expressing shock than posing a genuine question.

She joined the dots for me even though the amazing truth was gradually sinking in.

My emotions were all over the place. I felt at once shock, resentment, betrayal, disappointment, sadness and pride.

She was speaking continuously but I wasn't giving her my full attention as I was vainly attempting to process what I had been inundated by.

'Why didn't you tell me that you were pregnant? You should have told me that I had a kid?'

She did not have to think.

That had been well prepared.

'Look, I accept that I should have told you but we had gone our separate ways. I figured you might have felt trapped or felt forced to be part of a trio, which you had never banked on. I love kids and was not all that worried about being a single mum'.

The unsuspecting, chirpy waitress had returned with our soup and freshly cut sandwiches at that untimely moment.

I had just lost my appetite.

I felt that Suzi had been very high- handed and selfish with her decision -making.

She did not want me in her life.

'It wasn't your call to make', I insisted. Don't you think that I have a right to know that I have a son and that the young lad is entitled to know his father? For Christ's sake Suzi, he must feel that he has a waster of a dad, who has rejected him. What story have you fed him about me?' I demanded to know.

She was growing increasingly flustered and tearful. This encounter had been painful for her too.

'The poor lad is only coming nine. He doesn't need insecurity. My husband Hassan and Alfie are so close. He sees Hassan as his dad'.

I was very angered by this.

'I would have been there for him too if I had known. I have more entitlement to be in his life than this Hassan character from God knows where'.

I was becoming increasingly angry.

I felt cheated and mistreated at being written out of this child's life.

My tone grew more assertive and even borderline abusive.

Suzi was well able to defend herself and well able to go on the attack as well.

' Hassan is Iranian. He works as a doctor. He is a decent and kind man. We married three years ago and he took on the little kid as his own. He loves Alfie and Alfie loves him'.

That might have appeared lovely and dandy to her. It was far from right as far as I was concerned.

'But he is not his dad. Is he? He is bloody well my child and I have a right to be in his life.'

She took a moment before she spoke.

'I presume Danny, that you have a partner or a wife. Tell me do you have any kids?'

'No, I don't. Not yet anyway but she is anxious to start a family. But I have a kid with you and you robbed me of even the knowledge that I was a dad'.

We traded words like boxers in a ring might trade blows. It all seemed to be going around in circles. Then a question, which I should have thought of earlier, suddenly came to my mind.

'Well, you changed your mind about telling me about the lad. Why now? Has he begun to ask questions about me?'

She sat back in her chair and rubbed the emerging tears from her eyes with the back of her hand. She took a moment to compose herself. I was all ears and intrigued, to hear her explanation.

'Danny, I can understand your shock and I definitely can understand that you are angry with me. I have kept it simple for Alfie because of his age.

He has been told that his dad is a lovely guy who is away working on computers, which, by the way, really excited him. He and Mum split up some years ago but his dad will, one day, come back into his life when he was a bit older and they would have a great time together. He seemed happy with that' she added.

I suppose that reassured me, to a certain extent at least, that I was not being permanently excluded.

'So, I am to walk into his life someday, with an *iPad,* complete with a selection of gaming apps shouting 'Here's Daddy!'

She took the time to compose herself before resuming.

'Danny, the truth is that little Alfie is very seriously ill'.

I could see from her aspect that this was much more serious than a chest infection or whooping cough.

The awful thought struck me that he might be dying in the children's hospice. I feared that I was being brought in as almost a helpless stranger at the end of his life.

The situation was nearly as dire as that.

Suzi related the sad story of his ill health.

'You see, he was born with just one functioning kidney. He might have been lucky like so many others with just the one but that was not to be. He suffered one infection after another. That was the awful pattern. He has missed a lot of school time and has been in and out of the hospital for a long time now. Then it got more and more serious. He ended up on dialysis and that's where it's at now. A couple of weeks back, we were told that he needs a transplant and he needs it urgently. If he doesn't get one very soon, it could be the end for him'.

That terrible vista of this impending disaster broke down the strong wall of composure and objectivity that she had built to protect her. In front of me, she was no longer the woman who had callously kept a secret from me. She was simply, a mother fighting to keep her child alive and she had a request to make of me.

'Danny, I volunteered a kidney. However, when I was checked out, I learned that like poor old Alfie, I haven't two functioning kidneys either. I asked you here to see whether you would ever consider undergoing a test, to tell if you might be a suitable kidney donor? I know it's a huge thing to ask but if you are willing, there is a very good chance that you might be a suitable donor'.

I did not hesitate for a moment. I surprised her and even myself, by reaching across the table and touching her hand.

'Of course, I will do the test. He is my son, for Christ's sake. I can only hope that it's a suitable match and they can fix him up as soon as possible'.

She was greatly relieved and appreciative.

'Thank you, Danny! Thank you so much. You are a lifesaver, maybe even literally but even with a perfect match, the whole transplant process takes weeks and maybe several months.'

Both of us silently processed that likely scenario for a moment before Suzi spoke.

'You will have to discuss it with your…'

'Yea! I will talk with Lucy. Yea, I sure will but I can guarantee you that I will be doing that test come hell or high water'.

She seemed greatly relieved to have the burden of revelation and request off her shoulders.

'What do you think Lucy will make of your having a son?'

That was a question and a half and for the moment at least, I didn't want to go there.

'She will be sad about Alfie's plight. Yet, she will be even more shocked than I was to hear that I have a child. I know that she would like a kid herself but we haven't got around to it yet. It will go hard on her. Strangely, I already feel disloyal to her, even though I hadn't even met her when Alfie was conceived.'

She could appreciate that.

'Yea, I know. I was trying to put myself in her position just now and I know that I would be angry and resentful towards you, even though I know I shouldn't be.'

We spoke for a further few moments about our respective situations. She had abandoned the catering game and had started on her architectural career. While it was interesting to hear what she was doing, my mind was not engaged on that topic. The only thing that I could think of was that I was a dad and that my child desperately needed me. There was also the matter of telling Lucy. We said our goodbyes but not before we exchanged mobile numbers.

I paid for the uneaten food and made my way to the car park. I sat into my car and drove to the office. My mind was all consumed with these shocking revelations. I became lost in my thoughts and lost track of what I was doing, that is until the accident happened.

Chapter 8

The night before Danny's funeral, my house was full of family, friends and neighbours. All had come to offer sympathy and support. I knew most of the callers. Around ten o'clock, I had a surprise visitor. My sister had answered the door to a priest, who had requested to speak to me privately.

She showed him into the small study. He introduced himself as Fr. Eamon Dunne. He was on holiday from his parish in Nottingham, in England. It transpired that he had arrived on the scene of Danny's fatal accident. Danny was still conscious at the time. Fr. Eamon had prayed over him and sought to comfort him. I was so relieved to hear that Danny was not alone in those final moments.

Fr. Eamon had then followed the ambulance but had to leave the hospital, almost immediately as Danny had been whisked off to theatre. He had kept himself informed of developments and knew that Danny hadn't made it. His visit was not only to offer his sympathy but also to acquaint me with the fragmented conversation he had with my Danny, as he lay dying.

'Danny was drifting in and out of consciousness but he did mention your name 'Lucy' on several occasions. He specifically, asked me to carry his love to you. He must have felt that the end was close and he was anxious to let you know that he loved you'.

My tears started to flow once more, even though, by this stage, I should have had no tears left. This was the saddest message, which had ever been delivered to me but strangely it was also a heart-warming message. I was so glad that this priest took the time out to communicate this to me.

Almost as an after-thought, the priest mentioned something else.

'Danny also mentioned the name 'Alfie' on two occasions. Might that be a son?'

'No Father, he didn't or I mean, we don't have any children'.

'Well, a brother or friend, maybe?'

'No, Father. It was nobody in his family or his circle at all as far as I know and we have no pet. Danny did have a pet dog in his youth, which he worshipped. From my memory, I think its name was Rover.'

The priest smiled.

'I had a dog called Rover too. It's a popular dog name. Ah well, I suppose when you are in a traumatic situation and the oxygen to the brain is running short, one doesn't always make sense but I thought I should mention that to you too'.

'Thank you, Father! And tell me: did he appear to be in pain or was he crying out or what?

I was desperate to know and this was one man who could give me a definitive answer on this point.

The priest shook his head.

'No, there was no indication that he was in great physical pain. Perhaps the shock numbed him. Hopefully, it did. As I said, he had lost a lot of blood and he was lapsing in and out of consciousness. But when he was conscious, he was adamant that he wanted me to communicate his love to you'.

The priest declined my offer of refreshments. He took his leave, having promised to say a mass for Danny and for me.

'It must be some comfort to know that he loved you'.

'More than you can imagine, Father'.

'And I love you too, Danny and always will.'

Chapter 9

I was never a very religious man as regards worship but I had a certain basic faith. I believed in an afterlife, in which I would be reunited with loved ones, who had gone before me. The notion of a judgment of one's life, I had been less sure about. Just then, I was beginning to have concerns on that front. Might I be about to meet my Creator and Judge? The very thought filled me with terror.

By my estimation, I had led a reasonably good life. If life were a school or a college exam, I would be confident that I would squeeze in under the wire, hopefully with a few percentage points to spare. But what if one was expected to be better than mediocre? In that scenario, I could be in a bit of trouble.

As a youngster, I considered that I had acquitted myself reasonably well. We enjoyed a happy home life, all three of us and in all modesty, I believed that I played my part in that. I was not a boozer. I never took drugs and I was never a troublemaker. I worked hard at school. I worked equally hard on the land and I can't recall ever having any serious row, with either of my parents. I probably wasn't the perfect child but I was a pretty decent one.

In my twenties, there might have been a few black marks against me. I am not making excuses for myself but there were extenuating circumstances. I felt that Fate had dealt me a cruel hand. I sought comfort in physical pleasures. I probably drank more than I should and I became a bit of a womaniser. Anyway, I never believed that one's final judgment would come down to a box-ticking exercise.

What I was most guilty of was the sins of omission. It was more of what I didn't do. Looking objectively back on my life, I can certainly detect a selfish streak running through it. Things had to be done the way I wanted them to be done or I could be difficult. I think I was quite intolerant.

Where I felt I had really failed, was in my relationship with my wife. I was so blessed to have Lucy in my life. I hardly deserved that woman.

Lucy was a bright young girl, with a zest for life. She made friends easily. I was inclined to be a bit on the morose and grumpy side.

I could not have been much fun to live with. I didn't want her friends calling round. Maybe, my background was to blame. I was an only child and seldom had friends at my house. I valued my privacy too much.

It would have been very clear to any unannounced caller that I didn't want them there. Over time, only the brave and the foolish continued to call.

Lucy, being far more sociable than I, felt obliged to meet her friends away from the house. She enjoyed going out a couple of nights a week. She loved the theatre and the music bars at weekends. She kept fit down at the local gymnasium.

I also resented her going out without me, so more and more she began to stay at home. That could not have been easy for her. Her one sinful pleasure was tucking into a big greasy burger and chips in the takeaway on her way home. She always bought one for me too. I was more interested in stretching out in front of the television on week evenings and the weekends were 'wall to wall' sport for me. Lucy was not a great sports fan but she did not complain.

This was probably the reason, why I didn't see my faults in sharp focus. They say that a single man can go blissfully through life, not realising that he has any fault at all. The same might not be the case for a married man. I was lucky in that regard.

Lucy wanted to start a family, but of course, I selfishly kicked for touch on that one. Therefore, on a scale of 1-10, I would probably have given me a 2, for performance as a husband.

I was very concerned. The most unnerving thing about my predicament was the uncertainty of it all. I was being brought somewhere but I had no clue as to whether that was for good or ill. A thought suddenly crossed my mind. Maybe, I might be about to be reunited with my deceased parents. If I were to, I hoped that they were in a good spot. They deserved to be in the bright mansion, with the huge skylights onto the heavens. It would be great to have a reunion with them but not yet.

I was riddled with guilt about both Lucy and Alfie. I was heartbroken that I had never got to meet my little son or had the chance to improve his quality of life by donating a kidney to him. If only I had got an extra few months. If only I had started a family with Lucy. If only I had been a more considerate character all round. If only I had seen the traffic light change to red. There were too many 'if only' moments in my life.

After a prolonged period, my eyes were opened to a breath-taking display of colour and pattern, comparable only to a gigantic kaleidoscope. As if to shake me out of any unlikely complacency, I suddenly experienced a pick -up in speed. There followed a sensation of spinning. I can only compare it to being stuck in a washing machine, as it nears the end of its cycle. I was being spun at breakneck speed and tossed about. Some power or force, which I had never experienced before in my life, had now taken control of me. One thing was certain, I felt sure that I was coming near the end of this particular journey.

Chapter 10

Danny had broken a red light. The police told me so. I was so sorry to hear that. It would have been easier to blame someone else. However, what good would that do anyway? The poor, unfortunate lorry driver, who was moving on correctly on a green light did not have a chance of avoiding him. He had stood on the brakes but he could not prevent the inevitable. Thankfully, the lorry driver escaped physical injury but understandably, he was greatly traumatised. Eddie Kelly was the driver's name. He was a light, fine-boned man, and I figured that he was in his early sixties.

After the funeral mass, he bravely made his way through the crowd to sympathise with me. I bore no resentment towards him. How could I? If anything he was the innocent victim but Danny was the biggest loser. I could tell that he was blaming himself.

'I'm so sorry for your trouble, Mrs Keane', he began with the standard wording.

I got a shock, when he identified himself.

'I must confess that I was the driver of the lorry, that was involved in the collision, with your husband's car. Even though I had the green light, I'm kicking myself that I didn't see your husband coming.'

That took a lot of courage.

'Thank you for your sympathy but it wasn't your fault. The guards told me so already. You must try to put this behind you and get on with your life.'

'My life is it? My life is not what it was since my wife died four years ago. I'd be retired now, only that there is nothing at home for me'.

Once again, he reached for my hand.

'I swear to you, that I will pray every day and every night for your husband, as well as asking God to give you the strength to carry on'.

I thanked him again and promised to pray for him too, something which I fully intended to. He then moved away before melting into the crowd.

I found it physically exhausting and brain numbing to meet and accept the sympathy of so many people. Sudden or tragic death or the death of a young person always brings out a bigger crowd to a funeral. Everyone means well, but conversing with the sheer numbers, can be an incredibly stressful ordeal on the bereaved, both physically and mentally.

The funeral mass itself was solemn and respectful but it could not retain my attention. It was just like a humming sound in the distance.

An Emily Dickinson poem, which I had studied, for the Leaving Certificate, began to float into my mind.

*A Service, like a Drum -*
*Kept beating - beating - till I thought*
*My mind was going numb -*

After the cremation, we made the long car trip down the M4 to Sligo and then out by the lake to Dromahair, to finally arrive at the spot where we would scatter Danny's ashes. It seemed so apt and I was glad that I decided to cremate his remains rather than bury them.

We travelled, through gates, up to that small field in the townland of Ballyore. That field had been his favourite field, on what had been, the Keane family farm. Just a handful travelled on the last leg of the trip. That was what I wanted, an intimate little group. Kate and her husband Trevor were there. My brother Mark came along, as did my best friend, Karen Doyle. It was a really poignant moment when I turned the urn upside down and watched Danny's ashes settle onto the short grass. It was as if we were hitting the rewind button on his life and bringing it right back to the beginning.

To a casual observer, the field looked just like any ordinary little field in the countryside, except that it was just rockier than the others. As a townie, rural landscapes meant little to me. Therefore, it was difficult for me to relate to the young Danny spending delightful hours of solitude and reflection, in that very field. I tried to see it through his eyes but had failed miserably. It was as if the man had undergone a tremendous change, from being the boy to the adult Danny, whom I knew. My Danny had been an urban and indeed, urbane figure.

Although he adapted well to urban living, he was always a country boy at heart. Of course, there was no viable future in working the farm. The phrases 'North Leitrim land' and 'economically viable farming' never appear in the same sentence. Danny, despite his deep love for his home area never really had any desire to live on the land. He told me that he had seen too much drudgery, for precious little reward. Yet, that landscape and those childhood experiences had moulded him into the man he was. Even his everyday speech was peppered with rural imagery.

However, his background experience of open spaces and the resultant privacy meant that he found living in a housing estate very difficult. It seemed appropriate therefore that in death too, he had his own space, not crammed in close to some random neighbour, in a packed graveyard.

Chapter 11

I awoke with a shock. It was as if I had been dropped
unceremoniously from a height. It was all so confusing. I
looked all around me. My surroundings looked familiar but
there was a weird strangeness to that familiarity. I found myself
back in my favourite field, right behind my childhood home in
Dromahair. It was here that I planned my life and dreamed great
dreams for myself.

I imagined that I was winning Olympic gold for Ireland
in the 100 metres dash. I also dreamed of kicking the winning
point for Leitrim, in the All-Ireland Senior Football Final. I
don't know which was more unlikely.
Then, after my Leaving Certificate examination, I rehearsed my
performance on each paper, before attempting to predict my
mark on each of them and then calculate my overall points. This
scruffy little field had served as my den, my oasis of calm and
my sacred space, all rolled into one.

I suddenly felt even more disorientated. As my senses
recovered, I realised that I was still disembodied. I imagined
that my body was still back at the hospital. I wondered if I
would ever be reunited with it. I felt that I could not go on like
this indefinitely in this veritable wasteland. But I was helpless
to do very much about it.
 This was unchartered territory and this worried me. I wanted to
be at one with my body again and I wanted to be back with my
wife.

After some moments of feeling sorry for myself, I turned
to survey my new surroundings. I glanced around me. I couldn't
believe my eyes. How could this be? I took a second look in

case I was mistaken. There was no mistake. The spot where I had found myself was familiar to me. However, it looked different. What was different was the fact that I seemed to be viewing it in something even clearer than ultra-high definition.

What was I doing back there? It was years since I left the place, which had been the backdrop to my youth. It was as private and sheltered as a field could be. It was not overlooked by any houses or by the road or even by the mid-distance hills. It was private and secure and being there gave me the freedom to move around, play, sing or even shout, without fear of being overheard and embarrassed.

I would take a rug from the house and spread it on the grass there. No sun-worshipper treasured a golden Mediterranean beach more than I treasured that rushy and rocky field.

The field looked remarkably empty and eerie. There were usually a few cows or calves and sometimes a donkey, in that field but not anymore. These farm animals had grown used to me. We were, as much a part of their landscape as the overgrown hedgerows or the bare limestone outcrops.

However, time moved on as it always does and I went to college in Dublin. I graduated in Computer Studies. I had a brief stint in London before I returned to Dublin. When I married Lucy and set up home in the city, trips back to base became more intermittent. Then, after the tragic death of my parents, the place had lost its appeal. Pretty soon, I had sold on the property.

The death of my parents was without a shadow of a doubt, the worst period of my life and it was all so needless and so preventable. A large white plastic bag, which got lodged in the chimney, had caused their deaths. I don't know how it ended up being put onto the fire in the first place but it resulted in the carbon monoxide poisoning of my two parents on that fateful November night.

The postman had raised the alarm. He had a registered letter for them and when he got no reply at the door, he went around to the back door. Through a window, he saw them slumped in front of the television. This would have been highly unusual for them or any farming people at nine o'clock in the morning. When neither responded to his calling, the postman summoned assistance.

Mum and Dad did not suffer; they knew nothing about it. One evening they were watching the news and the next evening they were making the news.

I was devastated.

To be robbed of both parents, in one fell swoop, was too much to take. I could not get my head around it. They were only in their very early sixties and were full of life, with potentially decades left in them.

Being an only child, I had to take charge of all funeral arrangements. Some of my relations were very good to me, but our neighbours were the true heroes. They were brilliant. They rallied round, made tea and sandwiches, and opened their fields to facilitate car parking for the occasion. These neighbours also fed the farm animals and tidied up the place, to make it look its best for the callers.

I came close to giving up on life, as it did not seem to have much to offer. I was single and I had no notion that I could find happiness again. Time certainly dulls the rawness of the pain of loss but it never obliterated it for me, nor would I ever want it to. I grieved for them every day since, not with the same intensity as in the early days of mourning that sense of great loss never left me. From then on, I was a different man and I looked differently at the world. I realised how short and uncertain life can be, so I decided to make the most of it.

After some time, when I began to think straight again, I could not see the point in retaining ownership of the property at all. I know that this was because of the terrible associations there but there were practical considerations also. My workplace and my residential base were both in Dublin. The home place would be lying empty for most of the year. It needed year-round, human occupancy to remain dry and damp free. I hated to see it suffer any decline. After a brief period of reflection, I sold it to a young neighbour lad, who was planning to get married. To be viable as a farmer, he needed to extend his holding. This promised to be a convenient future home for him and the few acres of land with the house would help in that regard.

It seemed to work out for him and Dublin seemed to work out for me.

However, that was the backstory of my departure from the homestead but how did I now end up back in that field? What was happening to me?

I tried to retrace my movements or at least, rewind the tape that contained my memories. I remembered the crash, of course and in its aftermath, I recalled being in the hospital. After that, I seem to remember, being transported away from it. I also recalled the sensation of being pushed in a backward direction. I remembered getting sporadic glimpses of various stages of my earlier life. I never saw this field in any of those fleeting images.

Maybe I really had died. Maybe I had made the transition to the next life but if that were the case why was I back in my old life? Nothing made any sense at all.

Perhaps, there was some element of reincarnation involved. It might just be that I was being given my youth to live again. Maybe I had to set certain things right before I could travel any further. If that were the case, how could I do it without a body?

Just then a marvellous thought came to me. If I were back in time, then maybe, just maybe, my parents might still be living in the home place. Maybe I could speak to them again. This thought, daft and all as it may seem, wasn't any crazier than the weird and strange things that had already happened to me.

The house where I grew up was just beyond this field. Could my mum and dad be in that house right now, if I wandered down that way? I would dearly love to see them again, be a family again for another few moments. My dad had been a small farmer, who tended to his small herd of cattle and did his best to earn a meagre living from the impoverished soil there.

My mum assisted him and worked as hard outdoors as she did indoors. She cooked the meals, fed the animals, carried in the turf and coal for the fires and made the house a loving home. She and Dad had grown up close to each other and they had got married in their early twenties. They had been married ten years before I came along. It appears that they had given up hope of having a child and then, almost by magic, I came on the scene.

'You were an answer to our prayers', my mum used to tell me.

'God sent you to us and we thank Him every day since'. Dad would listen to her and tease her about God taking his time about it.

'You were never in much of a hurry,' he would say.

46

They never had another child.

Perhaps I missed out on not having brothers or sisters. I never knew anything else. It certainly made me independent and maybe just, a little self-centred.

Being an only child, my parents spoiled me. They had big plans for me. I was going to do better than they or their generation had done, in the absence of free education.

I had what was by most standards, an idyllic childhood, raised in a beautiful and peaceful area, doted on by fabulous parents. Whatever money they got from selling cattle or from selling milk to the creamery was earmarked for my future and me. Like many of their generation in rural Ireland, they sacrificed their own lives for their children. The scrimped and saved so that I would have a better life. But I was not always grateful. I had taken it all for granted.

Maybe I could remedy that now.

I sought to move in the direction of the house but I couldn't. The house was no longer there. There was no sign of the country road, no rolling drumlins, no mountains in the distance. I listened for some animal or bird sounds. There were none. All that existed in this place, in which I found myself, was this rocky, little field. It was as if this one physical remnant of my youth had been yanked away from its surroundings and cast adrift in an ocean of nothingness.

Chapter 12

On the night following the scattering of the ashes, we stayed with my brother Mark in Sligo. For me, this was coming home. It was where it all started for me. I did my melancholic reflection on where life had just taken me. I learned just how blessed I had been, up until then. The future however, seemed bleak and joyless even though the full enormity of the tragedy had not fully registered with me. It was as if Danny had gone away and would soon return. I liked to fool myself into thinking that he was away at a conference. I would wait for his key to turn in the front door or my mobile to ring and hear his voice telling me that he was on his way home. I was fooling nobody, not even myself. Danny was gone. He was not going to return now, nor at any time in the future.

My life would be empty without him. In these early days of bereavement, I kept myself busy. People were still rallying around to support me but gradually, the numbers became fewer and fewer. Soon I found myself alone in a silent, empty house, miserably reminiscing on the wonderful life I had enjoyed.

I grew up in Sligo town and although Danny lived only about twelve or thirteen miles away, our paths never crossed. Later we socialised in the bars and nightclubs of Sligo but he remained a stranger, until we met in a Dublin nightclub, several years later.

On that occasion, Danny Keane had been out on the town with friends and had a bellyful of beer on board. Alcohol always had the effect of making him more chatty and agreeable. Surprisingly, he was somewhat bashful in female company. The reason I agreed to go out with him was down more to his manly good looks than to his personality. I often wondered how things might have turned out if I had met the sober version of Danny Keane, on that night. I may never have gone out with him. Such are the quirks of fate!

Once I got to know the man, I could see beyond the bluster, right into his kind and decent heart. I had often heard that opposites make the best of matches and I can vouch for that.

As a very self-conscious person, who might even apologise for my very existence, I really admired a man who couldn't care less what others thought about him. Yet, he was never gratuitously insulting or hurtful to anyone but neither did he shirk from telling the plain, unvarnished truth. There was no nonsense about him. What you saw was what you got. That appealed to me.

Looking back, I can honestly say that I was never, ever bored in his company. That fact alone, spoke volumes.

He confessed that for him, it was love at first sight when he met me. As an unsure and self-conscious girl, that was great to hear. Danny always treated me like a lady. He showered me with flowers, chocolates and jewellery. That continued into married life. Long after the heady days of courtship, he would make a point of acknowledging my importance in his life. Every birthday, every Christmas, every anniversary or indeed every time he felt like it, he gave me a token of his love, usually featuring jewellery.

Danny had an enquiring mind. He loved current affairs programmes on radio and television and he would rarely miss the main evening news bulletin on television. I had precious little time for current affairs. Soap operas, courtroom dramas and medical programmes were more my thing. Television no longer holds the same interest for me. I often find myself, looking at the screen but yet my mind is not on the programme.

My sister Kate has been very kind. Even though she had her own commitments in England, she stayed with me for a week after the funeral so that when the funeral crowds melted away, I would still have some company. Despite her presence, I missed my Danny so very much. Each minute of the day seemed empty and pointless. I found it difficult to sleep. That was only to be expected. I declined my doctor's offer of sleeping pills to help me cope because I had to learn to cope with a terrible new reality. I would regularly lie awake until three or four in the morning. After a couple of hours, I would wake again; desperately hoping that Danny's death was just a bad dream. But no such luck, the cold, empty space was still there.

At thirty-six years of age, I was a widow and I was alone.

Chapter 13

I was in the field, which held so many happy memories for me but it was not in a context I could enjoy. I was alone. I felt lost and abandoned.

When I wasn't wallowing in self-pity, I was feeling anxious about Lucy and Alfie. Was she coping without me? There were so many things I wanted to help her with. She wasn't aware of some of my more recent investments but that might get sorted in time. Even the ordinary everyday tasks were a mystery to her. However, she was strong, she was clever and she was also very resilient.

I wondered how long Alfie might survive, in the absence of a suitable kidney donor becoming available. I didn't want the lad to suffer any more. I could not forgive myself for that momentary lapse in concentration, which had cruelly denied him his best chance for a suitable kidney.

As for my predicament, I felt sure that, this transition stage could not last for much longer. But what if it did? How long could I be expected to move aimlessly in a world that was only a pale reflection of one I once inhabited? There had to be something more to it. I might ordinarily have panicked at this stage but something inside of me told me that things would work out.

It was then that Tommie's face made a welcome reappearance. This time, I believed my eyes. I was greatly relieved. It was like an answer to a prayer. This familiar face was one, which understood me so well. We were 'kindred spirits' one might even say.

'You are still sweating about the small things', he said. 'You have to let go of all that. If you don't, there is no moving on for you'.

That was my first real indication that this limbo-style existence was not necessarily going to be permanent. But what was there to move on to? My mind jumped back to my primary school in Dromahair, when we learned about Heaven and Hell and indeed Purgatory. I wondered if I was in a Purgatory of sorts, being punished for some sins or omissions in my lifetime. But if I were being punished, then for what period had I to endure that punishment? I wondered whether that was what Tommie was referring to.

Tommie seemed to appear and disappear in quite a random way. It was like trying to *Skype* someone with a dodgy *wifi* connection. Pretty soon however he seemed to have fully made the connection with me.

'What am I doing here Tommie?' I asked.

'Well, it's bit like the train journey from Sligo to Dublin was in my time. You had to get out at Mullingar and change to another train for the rest of your journey. Well Danny, at the moment, you are stuck at Mullingar waiting to change trains. For you to go further, you have to clear that bloody head of yours of all that stuff that's keeping you from moving on.'

'What stuff are you talking about?'

'You have to leave behind your old life. You can't hold onto one life and try to move into another, no more than you could be alive and dead at the same time'.

'Jesus Tommie! I can't move on when I have so much unfinished business'.

He answered like a man who had heard it all before

'Yea, it's funny. So many arrive here with unfinished business even though we know all along that Death is heading our way'.

While that was true, it was of little value to me.

I asked him why I was back on home ground and wondered if it were his idea of making me feel a bit more at home.

'Nothing to do with me! You are here because the widow woman decided to scatter your ashes. She thought you might like it that way'.

Wow! That rocked me to the core.

'I was cremated?'

There was such finality to that.

'Yea, that's right, you went up in smoke and your good woman thought it would be nice to bring you back down to earth, as you might say'.

That was a Lucy thing to do. She was enduring her terrible loss but was still thinking of what I might like.

'So, I can kiss goodbye to being connected up to my body again', I added more in the way of a lament than a question.

'They are good on the bodywork here, I can tell you. There would be no bother at all in resurrecting that old body for you, if that is what is needed or even a younger edition of the same body.'

In that context, I had a question for my kindred spirit.

'Are you really Tommie? I mean the Tommie I knew. Have you still a memory of what happened in your time down below?'

'Yea, Danny boy, I am certainly the same old Tommie with the same old face', he smirked.

I think that his humour helped relax me somewhat.

Then, as if to underline that it was the same old Tommie, but in a fun-sized form, he referred back to my family tragedy.

'And it must have been horrible for you when your old pair passed. It was very sudden.'

'Are they here somewhere too?'

' Danny, even you can understand that I couldn't tell you that, even if I knew, which I don't '.

My parents had never done anyone a bad turn in all of their lives. I knew that if they weren't in for a good spot in the afterlife, I could forget about it.

I had a question.

'Tommie, you know those bad people, such as those awful tyrants, from the History books. Are they getting through to the next level'?

Tommie took a moment to consider his answer.

'Well, all I can say is that I haven't seen any of them around here. Although they might have sneaked in on my day off, if they are not down below, that is.'

'Tommie, It's all so weird and strange for me', I sighed.

'Ah of course it is. Any new place is different and it takes a bit of getting used to.'

His job with me, he confided, was to act as a sort of mentor or guide and help me sort out any issues, which might be preventing me from moving on to the next realm.

'You and I need to get our heads together and have a good chat'.

I chanced my luck with a bit of levity.

'Sure, Tommie, do you know any place around here, which serves a good pint?' I joked.

'No pints here, only spirits now!' he laughed, just as he would have done in life.

I felt sure that it was going to be an interesting chat.

In a moment, he was gone and I was left alone again to consider my plight. Soon, I felt very sleepy, as if I had swallowed a fist full of sleeping tablets. I was slipping deep into a slumber, the likes of which I had never experienced before. Clearly, something was afoot.

Chapter 14

For the umpteenth time, I wondered why Danny had been so distracted that he missed the red light. He was normally so alert to light changes and he knew that particular stretch of road very well.

The screen on his mobile phone had been shattered in the accident but the Garda investigators had checked the phone records to see if it had been used in the lead up to the accident. It had not.

I had often observed Danny grow agitated after quarrelsome encounters with various individuals, but once behind the wheel, his focus had always been on the road. One thing, which continued to puzzle me, was his reason for being out of the office. There was no diary entry for that trip, so it may not have been a business -related trip.

Whatever the reason, it mattered little now, except to satisfy my curiosity. Danny had been taken from me and taken so suddenly that I did not get time to say 'Goodbye'. Karen tried to console me by presenting a sudden death as being the lesser of two evils. She argued that Danny could have been left brain-dead, in a sort of death-in -life existence. That was true. It would have been a living nightmare for us. Should I be glad that he was dead? No way!

I would willingly and even joyfully have tended to his physical needs day in and day out for the rest of my natural life, just to have him with me. The pain of separation was the greatest pain of all. If I could, I would even have settled for just his breath in the room with me, and the feeling of his body close to me in bed. But, I knew for certain, such a limited existence would not suit Danny. It would be all or nothing with him. He could never cope with disability.

Some years ago, Danny broke his ankle while playing indoor soccer with some friends. He had his leg in plaster for six weeks. This had been a huge frustration for him. He felt helpless and emasculated because I had to become his driver. It nearly drove both of us crazy. He was a terrible patient and an even worse passenger.

For the duration of his immobility, Danny took to comfort eating. He put on one and a half stone in weight. This made him even more depressed and even gave rise to temper tantrums on his part. For some unknown reason, he had always harboured a particular dislike for fat people. He would always blame them for their weight problems. Now, he was becoming one of those people and he did not like it, not one little bit.

I think that it was a salutary lesson for him. Needless to say, when he was mobile again, he went on a crash diet and stepped up his exercise regime. Perhaps Karen was right, there are worse things than dying.

Chapter 15

It was Tommie's familiar voice, that restored me to consciousness. I no longer had any concept of time. It was so unnerving. My first thoughts then, as always, since my untimely departure, were on how Lucy was coping without me. I was also worried that Alfie may be paying a high price because of my momentary distraction, while driving. There were so many arrangements, that I would have made, had I known that she would be left on her own. Given a few months more, I could have had Alfie on a path to recovery.

Of course nobody knows what the future holds and we all act as if we have a limitless lease on life. This holds true even for people like me who think they are smarter than the average.

'What have you been doing with yourself?' he asked, almost as casually as if we had met by a country crossroads.

'If only I could do anything! It's terrible that I didn't do things when I had the chance'.

Tommie didn't reply. He just let me rant on about what I should have done to set Lucy up for independent living and do the same for my son.

I didn't know you had a son. Another young Keane lad setting out on life! 'Does he look like you?' he asked.

It was far from being the normal type of father-son relationship, which he would have been used to.

'Would you believe, Tommie, that I never laid eyes on him, much less met him. I have only seen his picture.

'Jesus!'

I could understand his shock.

I joined the dots for him. He seemed fascinated, especially about my having to come clean with Lucy. When I had finished my narrative, he took a sharp intake of breath.

'Jesus lad, that would have been a tricky circle to square with that wife of yours. It might sound strange maybe you are better off dead'.

I didn't believe that. I would certainly have taken a few hits from Lucy and our relationship might have been bumpy for a while but I would have tried to do the right thing. At least I would not be kicking myself when it would be too late like I was, just then. But there was no point in dealing with what might have been.

'How long do you think I'll be stuck here for? I asked.

His reply was puzzling.

'You decide that', he calmly stated.

I did not understand. What could he mean?

'All that stuff in your head has to be cleared before you can move on'.

'Move on to where?' I queried.

He was not about to reveal that to me.

'Now, Danny! That has to be a mystery to you. What I can tell you is that there are many lay-bys along the road you are travelling but the end destination could be a long way off.'

'Tommie, have I this right? Are you saying that until I forget about Lucy and Alfie, that I am stuck here?'

'Got it in one. The mind has to be clear for the spirit to make headway if you pardon the expression'.

That was that then.

I was going to be stuck here for the long haul.

'Yea, but Tommie, how can I put them out of my mind? She was the most important person in my life and I am really sad that I have left her high and dry. She wanted a baby and I would not give her one. Now, she is alone with no prospect of becoming a mother, in the medium term anyway'

I was talking away and Tommie seemed to be listening but what could anyone do about it?

'Lucy is a smart woman but she left all the financial and technical stuff to me. She is helpless in those matters. She doesn't even know her e-mail password or what cartridges go in what printer. And worse still, my young lad could die soon, if he doesn't get a kidney. And another thing, that poor lad probably thinks that his father walked out on him.'

Tommie seemed to understand and was probably frustrated that he could do nothing about it either. He was obliged to follow the set protocol. I knew that he would help me if it were within his power.

'Look here, Danny, I know it's tough about your son and I understand that you are worried about him. Anyone in your position would be worried but I don't buy that bit about your wife being badly set up. From what I can gather, she is set up better than most. You lost me when you were talking about e-mail. I don't even know what an e-mail is, much less a password. Is it a bit like saying *'Open Sesame*?'

'Yea, Tommie, something like that, only it is written down'.

He was not convinced of its importance.

'My generation seems to have got on without any of that but I take your word that it is important. And the whole thing about financial stuff, sure you know well that it will all get sorted out without you worrying your little, dead head. There is such a thing as death certificates and solicitors and all of that. It is not as if she is on her own, in that regard'.

I shook my head in exasperation.

' I know Tommie that it is hard for you to understand. I just can't move on when I have all that unfinished business especially with Junior.'

Tommie had always been a mild-mannered and courteous man but I could sense his growing impatience.

'Damn it! Danny, everyone coming this way has unfinished business of one sort or another. Nobody goes swinging through the pearly gates, pleased that they have tied up all loose ends.'

I didn't doubt it but I felt there was uniqueness to my case.

'Come on, Tommie, my case is different. Please help me out here, for old time's sake. You know the set up here. You are my guide after all'.

My approach did not look like it was going to pay off.

'Danny, I was doing my work as a guide, when I directed you to clear that head of yours. That is all; I was to do with you until you left all that worldly stuff behind. I was supposed to guide you further in your journey. However, you being stuck here has changed that.'

'Please, Tommie' I repeated.

' Come on, two Dromahair men together against the world and the hereafter.'

He became silent, as if he were mulling something over in his mind. I thought I detected a glimmer of a smile.

He left me after a few moments but not before he told me that he had to check out something. I felt that Tommie would help me if that were in any way possible and he did seem to be on some sort of inside track up here.

61

I was left alone again with my thoughts and my regrets. I wondered what Lucy was doing at that precise moment. I had no way of knowing whether it was night or day or indeed, what length of time had elapsed since my passing. As I considered her predicament, the thought came to me that she could never have guessed that I was stuck between two worlds. This was largely because I so wanted to assist her in coping without me. Least of all could she imagine that a son of mine was living within a few miles of her and that, even in death, I was desperately trying to help him. Such thoughts served only to reinforce my feelings of isolation and self-pity. I felt like breaking down in tears.

Thankfully, Tommie's face materialised once more.

'Danny, I told your story. I put your case. There is some sympathy up there for your plight because it could be a matter of life and death for someone. As I explained, selfish reasons don't cut any ice up here'.

It was the first and only piece of encouragement that I had received and I was hoping against hope that a solution could be found. However, I didn't want to build my hopes up. After all, what would a good result for me to be? I couldn't very well send down my kidney. If it hadn't been damaged in the accident, the cremation would have done it no good.

'What are you telling me, Tommie? Give it to me in plain simple terms.'

'What I am telling you is that every now and then an exception can be made for some poor soul, who desperately needs to do the right thing for another person, providing, of course, there is nothing in it for himself.'

I wondered what, if anything, he could do for me?

I was afraid to ask. Thankfully, it was going to be spelt out for me, by my old guide.

'The good news is that I have the authority to let you back to the world below for a set time but there would have to be a hell of a lot of conditions attached'
.

This was fantastic news. It sounded too good to be true.

'You mean that I can go back down where I came from and sort things out'.

'Yea, that's what I said, wasn't it?'

'And you said there were conditions….'.

'Yea, a barrow -load of them.'

'Like what, Tommie?'

'I have been given the go-ahead to allow you back to the previous world but, not as yourself. It has got to be as a very different person because the old you is dead and gone and there can be no going back as Danny Keane.'

'If I don't go back as me, what good am I to Alfie for a kidney match or Lucy either for that matter?' I demanded to know.

Tommie looked at me with a look of exasperation.

'Look here. You have to use your head. You will be let back into her world but only as a different person. Remember that you are not being let back there on a wild goose chase. A more knowledgeable hand that yours, might be at work so trust me. You are now being given a chance to sort out what can be sorted out and you better quickly learn what things cannot be sorted no matter what you do.'

This was incredible, so much more than I thought possible. It was difficult to get my head around it all. Was this just another one of my wild dreams?

For me going back, in any guise, was like hitting the jackpot. The best I had hoped was that somehow, someone could wave a sort of magic wand that could sort things out. I thought that in dealings with the omnipotent one, that this should be manageable but deep down I felt that it could never be. My curiosity was greatly aroused.

'Have I a choice as to what sort of individual I can be?

He scoffed at the very suggestion.

'You don't have a say in the world or up here either for that matter. You are being done an enormous favour, so don't look a gift horse in the mouth'.

'So I will probably go back as some sort of dork or simpleton'.

'Well, some might say, that would be nothing new to you', he laughed.

Even I joined in. I had been a bloody dork.

'Now Danny, pay good attention to me and remember well what I tell you'.

The fact that I was dealing with Tommie made me temporarily forget my circumstances and imagine it was an encounter with an old friend, back on earth. This was a huge source of comfort for me. If my guide had been a total stranger, I don't think that I would have chanced as much with another.

The rules of my return were about to be made clear to me in Tommie's inimitable way.

'You are going to go back, as a bloke, by the name of Reilly. Jack Reilly!'

'Wow, living the life of Reilly!' I ventured.

'Listen more and talk less', he replied, by way of admonishment.

That was something I had never envisaged. They could have decided that I might come back as a girl. That might have been more difficult for me to pull off successfully.

'And you will work as a schoolmaster in a primary school, teaching nine-year-olds'.

'Bloody hell, Tommie', I blurted out. God was laughing at my expense. I hadn't much time for men in primary education, well, let's just say that I didn't see them as being a very manly lot.'

Tommie's face took on a really serious aspect.

'Danny, if you don't want to be that bloke, then you can stay where you are but let me know now, before we all waste our time'.

'Jesus, Tommie, is there any chance I could be a carpenter or a plumber or an engineer, someone who does real work?'

He was adamant.

'Beggars can't be choosers! Being allowed to return means that the price you pay is always going to be a bit on the steep side.'

'You mean there could be more than that being demanded of me.'

'Well, for a start, he's probably not going to be a looker. And come here, I want you. Did you ever know a girl, by the name of Karen Doyle?'

'Yea, I know her. She is a good buddy of Lucy's but she would not be my cup of tea'.

'That's a pity because you are going to be her boyfriend', he declared.

'You are shitting me! Tommie. Tell me this is a joke. For fuck's sake! Me and bloody Karen Doyle!'

I disliked the woman because invariably, it was she who would be on the phone to Lucy for ages each evening. She was also likely to pay lengthy visits to the house on a few occasions each week. Karen Doyle always seemed to be monopolising my wife.

I really resented her.

Tommie was not spoofing.

'It's no joke at all. As I said, it is always the opposite of what a bloke wants. You didn't expect to be a boyfriend of Lucy's now, did you? Or an escort for some contestant in the Rose of Tralee?'

'Well no, Lucy wouldn't be up for another boyfriend so soon? I mean…I hope…would she?'

'Danny, you know her better than I do. And anyway, it's six months since you have been gone and who knows, she might be lonely and ready for a bit of male company. They say that a dead man is no good to any woman.'

That remark put things in some sort of perspective for me.

Six months since I passed over. Wow, bloody wow. I wondered what that meant for Alfie and his dialysis.

The thought of Lucy with another man haunted me. I didn't think that she would have moved on in six months, loneliness or no loneliness.

'And do you mean that I will just materialise there, like in that film about the bloke with no past?'

He seemed a bit impatient with my attitude and constant questioning.

'You are dealing with a crowd up here, Danny, who can do anything at all. The impossible is what they specialise in. There will be no doubt at all but you will be accepted as this Jack Reilly character, which comes with a past to match. There are a few restrictions that you will have to live with but you just might be given a few extra powers too just to balance things out'.

'Superhuman powers, do you mean? I asked.
'It will all become clear in good time.
My appetite had already been whetted.

Chapter 16

I imagined Danny came back to me last night. I was really
restless and only half asleep, when my nose detected an
unusually strong smell in my bedroom. There was an unusual,
yet pleasant smell, not unlike that of fresh flowers. I never put
flowers in a bedroom. I glanced at the digital alarm clock. It
told me that it was 3.10 a.m. I absentmindedly glanced around
the bedroom as I had done on countless occasions, over the
previous weeks. I couldn't believe what I was seeing. My heart
skipped a beat. I saw Danny sitting in the red-upholstered
armchair, which served both as a chair and as a makeshift
clotheshorse.
Danny was smiling across at me.
I wanted to speak but was too shocked to do so. I was not
afraid. I was delighted.
'Hello Lucy! I just wanted to look in on you and tell you that I
love you. I also want you to know I will always look out for
you'
Those words were so comforting. I could feel the knot, which
had gathered in the pit of my stomach, beginning to slowly
loosen.
'Lucy, I know you miss me but you have to move on with your
life and make the most of it'.
I found my tongue and was able to tell him that I would always
love him too and that I missed him so very much. He smiled
and blew a kiss at me. Then he was gone.
I sat bolt upright in the bed. I could feel my blood run cold. I
wondered what on earth had just happened. Soon, I was
hyperventilating. I began to panic. I did what I had done so
often as a kid, whenever I was scared. I lay back down in the

bed and covered my head with the duvet. I dared not look again. I hoped that sleep would come to my rescue.

I must have drifted off. The next thing I remembered was being awakened by the high-pitched sounds of feral cats fighting outside on the street. I silently cursed them. I checked the time. My alarm clock's display read: 2.35 a.m.
What the hell was going on? I double-checked the time on my mobile phone. The clock was right. I had just been dreaming when I imagined seeing the later time.

I felt bitterly disappointed as in the cold light of day, I realised that Danny had not come back to me. It had been nothing more than my over-active imagination. I felt so cheated. The thought of his returning had lifted my spirits. It was like dreaming of winning the lottery only to awaken to find your purse empty and more bills on the doormat. I felt worse than I had done for weeks. The whole experience just deepened my misery.

In the past, I had often been alone in the house before and for prolonged periods but it is very different when you know that your loved one is never going to return. I kept hearing things. On several occasions, I had convinced myself that someone had managed to get into the house but no one had. I had my house alarm on *Home* setting every evening. I took to leaving the radio on in the bedroom and the television in the living room, to help banish that eerie silence. I had lost interest in watching TV soaps, going for walks and surfing the Internet. I had made a conscious decision not to drink alone in the house. I thought that was wise and I was determined to abide by it.

There was too much time for brooding. I had good memories but I got precious little comfort from recalling happy days together with Danny. I felt cheated, cruelly cheated.

Danny had been taken from me. My life had been ruined. All around me there were wives, whose husbands were older and still with them. Why was my young husband taken from me? I wanted to scream at times. I wanted to run out into the street and scream at the world. I have to admit that I wondered how long I could put up with this death- in -life- type existence.

The fine summer weather was doing its best to cheer me outside but I was not tempted out. Ordinarily, I would be out on my daily walk and the occasional weekend cycle but I stayed indoors. The god, who sent the sunshine, was not my god any longer. I sought the darkness. There was a certain comfort in seclusion. Like a cat licking its wounds, I was nursing my wounds of grief. Of course, I had to go out to work. Bills still had to be paid.

When preoccupied, as was often the case in the office or away on business, I was fine. Danny had never been a part of my day there, so I did not miss him there. I threw myself into my work. Andrew, my immediate superior was particularly kind to me. He had been with me in the hospital and he kept looking in on me, assuring me that he was always there and would be a very willing ear if I should need anyone to talk to. If I wanted time off, that was fine by him too. Additional time on my own was the last thing that I wanted. I needed to be out of the house.

In the past, at the end of a working day, I would make a mad dash home. I would be planning a dinner for two, or a meal for some friends. Now, there was no hurry. There was nothing to go home for. I saw it as being less of a home and more of a shelter. The beating heart is gone from it.

That was where all the terrible reminders resided.

Even though it was just six months since Danny's death, it felt much longer. I was really hurting.

My work colleagues had been really sensitive towards me but had now returned to their default setting. They had moved on. I was not yet coping

My friend Karen was pushing me to socialise more. This was from the very best of intentions as she is kind and attentive.

We had gone out for a couple of meals together and dropped into a city pub for a couple of drinks afterwards. It was of no benefit, as it merely served as a reminder of what I was missing. It could not have done her much good either. I was just a physical presence with her. My mind was elsewhere and I could see no change in that situation for a long time to come. I was conscious of that emptiness in my life, all of the time. That emptiness was the absence of my beloved Danny.

Frequently I would hear something or maybe something happened at work and I would immediately think that I should tell Danny or ask him if he had heard the particular news. That familiar sinking feeling would return the moment the realisation hit that he was not there any longer. I still kept the text message I sent on the day of the crash. He had never got to read it. I regretted not having saved one of his many voice messages but Karen tells me that I might be better this way. I am not sure.

I felt embarrassed that Karen was lavishing so much attention on me. She had her own life to live. Karen was a single girl and would love to meet a man. She needed to have a social life and she needed a companion on a night out.

I did not have the heart to be her companion. Indeed, I would surely put a dampener on any evening. She had been on dating websites for professional or educated classes. That sounds so snobbish and exclusive but maybe that is what was needed. She needed someone who would be her intellectual equal. Karen had also been used to her creature comforts. He dad had been a prosperous real estate agent and her mother was a Building Society manager. There seemed to be plenty of money for Karen to spend. She had travelled all around Europe. She was on a reasonably good salary in the Civil Service and I could not see her trade in that lifestyle for a less privileged one.

There was one lad, Martin, who stole her heart. He and she had dated for some time, when they were in their early twenties. However, Martin went to work in London's Financial City district. I think that he may well have been the one true love of her life. It was always going to be difficult to settle for less.

But she was on a dating site and she had already been introduced to a few nice guys. Up to now, nothing came of it. I felt she had to persevere with it. She was only thirty-two years of age but to listen to her, one would think she was forty -two.

Sadly, her self- image had taken a bit of a hit also. It was difficult for me to view another woman from a man's perspective but I would say that Karen was an attractive woman. She stood about five foot eight inches in height, two inches more than I am, with wonderful straight hair, which looks so good, whether up-styled or down. She needed to get herself out there, meet the right man and settle down together and start a family.

I urged her to persevere with the dating website.

Chapter 17

I must have been unconscious for some time because the next thing I experienced was a sensation of hitting the ground with a thud. It was exactly like the sensation, which had preceded my landing in the small field, behind my childhood home. I was puzzled.

When the fog lifted from my brain, I found myself sitting in, what appeared to be, the lobby of a hotel. It had a familiar look to it.

I looked all around. There was a partially frosted window behind me. From my seated position, I could not see out onto the street, so I stood up to get a proper view. The midsection was frosted, evidently to preserve the patrons' privacy. When I stood up, I could see the *Luas* light rail trams. I knew immediately that I was back in Dublin city. More specifically, I was in the foyer of a hotel just off St. Stephen's Green. Apparently, I had successfully made the return trip. My heart quickened with expectation and relief.

We had often used this hotel as a meeting place in town. There was always ample seating in the lobby and nobody minded one waiting there.

But why was I there? What was the plan?

I soon became aware that for the first time in six months, I had a body again but it couldn't be the old one, which had been cremated or could it? I could see my torso and my hands, which curiously, held a glass of sparkling water. I wanted to know what I looked like so I decided to head to the downstairs toilets, where I could find a mirror. As I got to my feet, I became conscious of someone moving in alongside me. When that person spoke I was a bit disconcerted.

'Where do you think you are off to?'

Who was it but my old neighbour and spirit -guide, Tommie? Who else?

He looked different. He was no longer just a face. He too, had taken a body. It was not the body that I had always associated with him. I recalled that he had said that one could never return as oneself. At least he was being consistent. What was sauce for the goose seemed also to be sauce for the gander!

Tommie could easily be mistaken for any of many middle-aged businessmen, who were such a common sight in the city. I felt so pleased to see him. I had to remind myself that we were two ghosts, who had come back to the earthly realm. There we were, anonymous and unnoticed among the shoppers and business people of the capital. I wondered too whether more of these people walking purposefully passed were returned spirits.

I remembered Tommie's dislike of urban environments.

'Dublin wasn't a place you were ever too familiar with, Tommie. Was it?'

' North Leitrim was my area and I was more than happy to stay there'.

I too could see the attraction of the home place but economic necessity makes migrants of so many.

'Tommie, I was just thinking there, that returned spirits could well be used to boost the population of the county'.

He laughed. 'I doubt it, Danny. Even if we could, we would not have a ghost's chance of being included on the census form.'

Tommie was primed to fill me in on a few important points about my new identity and what I could do or more importantly could not do. My more immediate concern was the rather vain one, of how the new me looked.

I have to admit that being back in the land of the living, I momentarily forgot about my predicament. I suppose that I imagined that somehow, things would be all right, without really appreciating that I was still separated from my Lucy and no matter what happened with my new persona, that we could never be together. My heart sank and it was clear that Tommie had noticed this.

'Danny, you look as if you have lost a pound and found a penny but remember that you signed up to this. Now, you have to make the best of it or otherwise we might as well head back this very minute. Do you want to help out people or don't you?'

I was feeling sorry for myself yet I had to recognise that I was lucky enough to get a second chance to sort out my affairs. I could see Lucy again and I might be in a position to help her. I could see my son for the first time and hopefully, allow him to live a normal life. What was there to be sad about?

I had to focus on the challenge ahead.

'Well, Danny, as I mentioned earlier you will have some special powers that nobody down here can have. I hear that you already had an experience with one of those'.

I would be able to move about unseen. I had that particular experience, just before I died when I witnessed Lucy in the little hospital oratory.

There was more.

'Now that power to be invisible is just for up to one hour in any week, one-hour maximum', he stressed.

Tommy called this *the invisibility shield.* This would be valuable for me but with a one -hour limit, I was not likely to abuse the power.

I would essentially be under the control and direction of the powers upstairs.

I wondered what else I might have in the line of superhuman powers.

My thoughts seemed to have been anticipated.

'And you will always have the knowhow needed for whatever job might be handed to you.'

'What do you mean? I asked.

'You won't have to learn anything before you teach. That knowledge will be pre-programmed into that head of yours, together with your back story and all of that stuff', he explained.

That was some relief anyway.

That was much to absorb. I was processing some of those points when Tommie warned me that I couldn't, in any way whatsoever, give even the slightest clue about who I was or I would be back in the rock field quicker than I could say 'Rest in Peace'.

'You are being allowed back to the mortal world so that you can help your young lad deal with his problems, not to fuss over your young widow. She will survive without you but feel free to help her where you can. Remember it is another chance you are getting, with no guarantees. Do you hear me, another chance, just that? There are no guarantees that anything will work out, just another chance being given to you.'.

I nodded my understanding of this.

He was not finished yet.

'There can't be any funny business between you and Lucy or with Alfie's mother either. That means absolutely no messing or sniffing around either of them. They can never even suspect who you might have been. I think you get my drift. If you want that sort of action, Karen is your girlfriend. Remember!'.

I tried not to think of that. I would have loved to attempt to woo Lucy again and maybe eventually give her that baby she so desired. It was disappointing that I couldn't even go there.

'So Danny lad, the bottom line is that you do what you came back to do, get it over with and get back. Be warned that you are not being gifted a second life span'.

'I wasn't even given that first time around so maybe we might average things out'.

Tommie seemed to grow impatient with me.

'It is not about you. It is about your son and less so about your widow. Do what you can for them before you find yourself back above with nothing else to show for it'.

'How quickly do I have to get moving?' I wanted to know.

'Things will be different to what it used to be for you. You won't be able to decide when you can do everything. The crowd upstairs will arrange things to happen in a certain way and at a certain time and not until that time is right. You can't just go out tonight and sort things out. From what I hear, Lucy is gone home for a while'.

It was great to get the update on Lucy. From my point of view, I saw assisting her as being equally important to helping Alfie. I had imagined that there might be a few wise boys biding their time before they might make a move on her. I intended to sort them out.

Tommie had one final warning for me.

'Anyway, remember there can never be any suggestion that there is any funny, supernatural business going on. Any slips on your part, and it's all over.'

As I absorbed all of this information, my thoughts turned back to my new self, my new body with which I would present myself to the world.

I needed to get a look at myself.

' Tommie, I need to nip down to the toilets'.

He looked aghast.

'No, you don't need to go unless someone has badly slipped up with the design.'

I attempted to explain.

'No, not to use the toilet! I need to look at myself in the mirror. Remember, I don't know yet what I look like'.

He had forgotten about that.

'Well, all right then, but I can tell you that. You are as you already guessed, a weedy-looking bloke, a bit gawky-looking, with sandy hair and kind of crooked teeth. How does that grab you?' he asked.

From our previous discussions, I knew that he was not joking.

'It is a bit disappointing, to say the least but I still wanted to see for myself.'

I left Tommie where he was and went to have a good look at myself in the bathroom mirror. It was not a pretty sight. I had become that weedy looking bloke, with lank sandy hair and uneven, yellowing teeth. I was also about three inches smaller than I had been in my previous incarnation. I was a right puny, little bastard, the sort I had nothing except contempt for.

This was a terrible disappointment. Then again, it was hardly a surprise. Being allowed back always came at a high price. I had to be focused and positive. I was there to be of assistance to others, not to further my own agenda.

Back in the lobby, I sat down beside Tommie and gave him a rueful smile.

'Jesus, Tommie, I am a right looking prick', I lamented.

'Yea, tell you the truth, things are always that way, so don't take it personally'.

'Not much of a babe magnet!' I lamented.

Tommie seemed impatient with me.

'That won't matter and it won't hold you back with Karen. Anyway, any funny business with anyone else and you will find yourself lifted out of there before you can drop your trousers. And before I forget, this Karen girl and you have just met online, whatever that means. And you are meeting up with her tomorrow evening.'

This was enough to bring me back to earth. I shook my head at Tommie in absolute bewilderment.

'Welcome home, Danny'.

Chapter 18

I had to take last week off work. It was six months since Danny passed on and it felt as if it were only six days away. I was not improving. I missed my Danny so much. I was panned out emotionally and physically, so I decided to take a week off work and head down to Sligo for a change of scene.

I needed to get away from Dublin, from work and from the memories that haunted our house. Andrew was showing an inordinate interest in my welfare. He even assigned some junior colleagues to lighten my workload. I also had carte blanche to head home, whenever I felt overwhelmed.
I was uneasy with his constantly reminding me that he was always there, as a shoulder to cry on. I wasn't a girl who wanted to cry on anyone's shoulder. My crying was done after work and alone in the privacy of my living room or bedroom. Nothing now seemed able to distract or engage me.

It felt strange to be back in my old room. Even though it had been redecorated, it still felt like my bedroom. The wardrobes were now practically empty. In the past, I had those same shelves full of my *Barbie* dolls. They were all sitting comfortably on the shelves. My dresses, jeans and tops had to be content with hanging out on the rails.

I had the best week's sleep since my love passed away. Danny had no connection with this room, so there were no ghosts there. It was as if I had retreated to an earlier, carefree stage of development and it felt safe and secure.
If only I could rewind time.

During my week at home, my brother Mark and I took a trip around Lough Gill to Dromahair. I wanted to visit the field where I had scattered Danny's ashes, back in February. The ashes were well dissipated by now and the grass had grown over anything, which remained. Nevertheless, I felt that there was a part of Danny still there. I had to visit it one more time.

I wanted to walk into that field alone. Mark seemed to understand. He waited in the farmyard, chatting to the owner, who permitted me to visit the field, whenever I felt like doing so.

It was as if Danny was in the field with me. I had such a strong sense of his presence that I began to speak aloud, to him.

*'Danny if you can hear me, I trust that you are at peace. I miss you dreadfully. I like to think that you are still with me in spirit. It would be great if you could give me a sign to show that you are with me but then again, that would scare the daylights out of me. I'm coping as best I can.*

*I am told things will get easier with time passing but it's early days yet. I miss you so much. I even miss the annoying things about you, like when you would open the dishwasher before the cycle ended.*

*I know that you would want me to be strong. I have to admit that there are times, when I wished that I had been killed along with you. I will carry on, and somehow, I will get through this.*

*Sleep tight Danny and you are always in my mind. Love you forever'.*

I dried up my tears, before walking back to the parked car. On that day, I sensed that something had changed in me. I felt different. It was as if my load had been in some way, lightened.

Maybe I had released the pent-up feelings of pain and hopelessness, or maybe, Danny was beginning to work his magic.

I appreciated Mark taking the time to drive me out. I offered to drive the return leg, if he fancied a pint in the village. He didn't need any persuasion.

As it was such a fine, late- August day, we took our drinks outside. We sat on one of the rustic benches there. Alongside us, a small group of continental visitors chatted and took pictures. As Mark sipped his frothy pint, I sipped on my mineral water and just took in the scene. It was certainly a far cry from the hustle and bustle of Dublin but it had its own appeal.

I bought Mark a second pint. We sat and chatted. Even Mark remarked on my improved mood.

'Yes, I still miss Danny so very much but I think the pain has become that little bit more bearable'.

'Good on you girl, I'll drink to that', he said.

Chapter 19

I was gradually and incrementally learning how things were going to work for me in this second coming. I was slowly learning that the world did not revolve around me. I was in this world, not in a lead role but purely as a supporting actor. I was slowly becoming aware of my own vanity and self-centredness.

Visiting to my former workplace was a sobering experience for me. I observed my former work colleagues, beavering away as usual. The atmosphere in the office was as always, light-hearted and cheery. Someone else now occupied my office. It seemed to have been a seamless transition. It was as if I had never been there.

I wondered whether any of my possessions had survived the inevitable cleanout.

I remembered when old Jim Watkins left the office in an ambulance, never to return, his personal effects had been tidied up and deposited on a shelf in the Photocopying Room. I decided to have a quick look there.

There was nothing in there for me.

I got a glimpse of my ex-boss Bernard. He was always fighting the flab and seemed to have put on a little weight since I had last seen him. He was in there chatting to Myra, the office administrator. They were making plans for an upcoming office party. Both seemed to be quite animated about it.

Going back into the main office space, I saw Paul, my best buddy, in the office. He was on the phone to a client and he was chatting away with his spectacles resting on the table alongside him. I would have loved to go up and playfully slap him on the back and ask him: 'How is she cutting?' as I had done countless times before. If there were one guy who would most likely miss me there, it would be Paul.

I couldn't resist the temptation to play a trick on him. As he removed his glasses while taking a call, I took them from the desk and put them dangling from a *Chelsea FC* team picture, that he had on his wall. Always a Blues supporter, he travelled to Stamford Bridge two or three times a year to see them play. I travelled with him on one occasion. We had a mighty time there. Paul was a great guy to socialise. He would be the life and soul of the upcoming party.

I wondered what lasting impression, if any, I had made in that employment. Sure, I did what I was paid to do but what did my workmates really think of me?

Whatever their opinion of me might have been, it was too late to do anything about it now. I had been consigned to the past and I had no relevance there since February 14.

That car crash cut me off from my career, my friends and most importantly my little son and my wife. I could only operate now when the higher powers facilitated it. That was so frustrating. I felt worthless. I was now little more than a remotely -controlled device.

I must have been out for some time, because when I opened my eyes again, I was back home or more correctly, I was back on the street, outside of my home. I waited for some time. Familiar faces passed by. I could see them but of course, no one could see me.

My new heart nearly stopped beating, when I observed the love of my life drive up the little suburban road. She had her jacket off and I could see that she was wearing sunglasses.

My old body had gone up in flames but my heart clearly went on. It beat so fast and so strongly, that I thought she might hear it beating. I was out of mind with delight. For a moment, I forgot myself and ran to embrace her. I wanted to grab her, hold her tight and assure her that I was back to take care of her.

But at that moment I was nothing to her.

My beloved Lucy was standing just inches away from me in her dark blue, work suit and yet I might as well have been in a different world.

I was nothing to her.

I cried angry, bitter tears as I followed her into the house.

Nevertheless, I was appreciative of getting another glimpse of her. I was desperate to remain in her company for as long as I could. Unfortunately, I was on a timer and it was already counting down the minutes.

As was her routine, she tossed down her handbag, keys and sunglasses onto the living room table, before walking to the fridge. A sip from a chilled bottle of water seemed to do the job for her thirst. She exhaled loudly, a deep sigh of relief, at having made it to the end of another week.

Before kicking off her shoes, she partly filled the kettle with water, just sufficient to make her a cup of tea.

She poured the boiling water onto a teabag, which she had placed in a small white cup. I had always been a mug man but she preferred her tea out of the china cup. A root in the snack- press yielded her a fun-sized chocolate snack, which she put in her trouser pocket. She took the black, sugarless tea into the living room. I have to admit that there was nothing distraught or melancholic looking about her. I heard no mournful sighs and saw no tears. Lucy appeared to be getting on with her life, a life that was without me.

While I would have hated to see her in a distressed state, I have to admit to a tinge of disappointment at her apparent ease in moving on. After all it was just eight short months since the death of her husband.

A quick flick through the channels brought nothing more than momentary distraction to her until she selected an unwatched episode of *Grey's Anatomy*.

Some things never change.

As she settled down to view the recording, I sat alongside her and feasted my eyes on the face I can't forget. I did not have endless time, so I had to look elsewhere, if I wanted to make life a bit easier for her by sorting out some issues.

I left the living room and wandered down to the Study. This was where I kept most of my important papers. I opened my expandable file folder.

As expected, some important documents were missing. Either the solicitor or accountant had presumably requested them.

There was still the question of the *Managed Fund* documents and the recent Life Assurance policy I had left in an old attaché case. This was well hidden, behind the suitcases, at the bottom of the airing cupboard. It was a stupid place to keep them. I moved the suitcases around until I found the attaché case. The documents were as I had left them two years previously.

Those documents needed to go to our solicitor. I would get a large envelope from our study and post them on my way out.

With the clock running down, on my invisibility shield, I took a few moments, to mooch around the house. Our bedroom was unchanged in any significant way. I pulled open my wardrobe door and was delighted to see all my clothes still hanging there.

I may have been gone but I was not forgotten. At least, that had been a little boost for me. I took a quick look at her wardrobe. It was, as always, neatly arranged. I shed a tear as I recalled seeing her in those very pieces. I ran my hand tenderly over the garments. I then took a look in the overhead press. This was where she kept her scarves and her handbags.

I lifted a light-blue, silk scarf from a shelf and held it close to my nose.

It still carried her fragrance upon it.

I decided to bring it with me, as a souvenir of happier times together.

I looked at the bed and tried to recall Lucy, lying beside me.

I had so many memories but was sad at the thought that never again would we curl up together on that king-sized bed.

The pain of separation was almost unbearable. I desperately wanted to communicate with her but that was not to be.

Just as I had taken a memento of her with me, I was anxious to provide her with a reminder of me, and our time together. Having considered my options, I removed a pair of socks from my sock drawer, rolled them into a ball and tossed them under the bed. The next time, she lifted the bed to hoover under it she would be reminded of me. It was a small thing but I hoped that it might prompt pleasant thoughts of me.

I noticed some sleeping tablets on her bedside locker. They were new to me. On the dressing table rested her pink *Guess* handbag. I had a quick look inside. I saw that she had received a replacement credit card, as the old one, rather like me, had recently expired. I decided to do what I always did on such occasions. I returned to the study and using my old laptop, I updated the bankcard details and expiry dates on *Amazon, eBay* and *Pay Pal* as well as her *Apple* account. She frequently used those websites for purchases. I also topped up her toll bridge account, to ease her passage, as it were.

My time in the house was almost up. I had to make tracks.

I returned to the living room. Lucy was still watching TV. I blew a loving kiss to her and I bid her a silent adieu.

The life we shared together was over. It was so sad and so final. We could never be together again, not in this world anyway.

I would never be part of her life again but I vowed to make a positive impact on it.

Chapter 20

Last night, Andrew asked me out for a drink. It was 'purely as friends', he stressed.

He is no friend of mine. He is my boss. That is the extent of his relationship to me.

He had been very attentive in recent times and I had been half-expecting such a move. I was inclined to decline the invitation but Karen twisted my arm a bit and pushed me to agree to it. I made it clear to Andrew that my grief was still very raw and it was much too early to even consider a new relationship. He seemed fine with that.

We settled on Thursday night. I opted for the smart casual look, featuring my skinny white jeans, navy blazer and crisp white shirt. I did not want to bare too much skin, in case I got him too excited.

Andrew had hired a taxi. He was dressed casually but smartly. Labels seemed to matter to him. He was dressed in a casual *GANT* shirt and beige *BOSS* slacks. He looked more relaxed than he had ever looked in his tailored office wear. He looked quite well.

I had grown used to his quiet ways and was not unduly concerned with the odd gap in conversation as we sat together, on our journey into the city.

The taxi dropped us off at *Stephen's Green Shopping Centre* on the edge of the pedestrian area.

Andrew paid the fare, while I stood on the footpath trying to figure out, where we might be going.

'It's just up here here', he said, pointing in the direction of the trams.

'Great, I can't walk far in these heels', I responded

As we strolled up the street, I was beginning to narrow down the possibilities. In a moment or two, we are at the door of *The Fitzwilliam Hotel*.

The lobby of the hotel was always an ideal meeting place and Danny and I often used it as a rendezvous. It was always a welcoming place and it was very close to large car parks.

I sensed that Andrew was nervous. I wasn't but I was apprehensive. I did not want to socialise with my boss. However, I could not afford to be rude. I decided to put my reservations to one side try to live in the moment. I would grin and bear it.

We took our seats in the sparsely populated bar. A well-mannered young waiter took our orders. He wanted *Hendricks's* gin and *Club* Tonic Water. He was certainly a man who knew his brands. I asked for a *Sancerre.*

Over the course of the evening, I discovered that Andrew was a very shy man.

There were long silences and periods of awkward conversation but those did not bother me.

However, over a period of time, he began to converse and seemed keen to be expansive. Apparently, he needed the alcohol to loosen him up and reduce his inhibitions.

He talked about himself and his background. More interestingly, he talked about his marriage breakup.

'Yea, it was a tough time. We were growing apart and living separate lives. I have to admit, that towards the end, the atmosphere in the house became toxic. In the end, we both realised that the best thing to do was to cut our losses and get on with our lives'.

I could see the sadness in his eyes.

I was slow to offer an opinion and so he continued.

'Thankfully there were no children to be traumatised by it all. Children tend to be the big losers when a marriage breaks down'.

'You are certainly right in that', I ventured.

'But who knows what fate has in store for me? As far as I'm concerned, the past is the past and the future awaits'.

His words were suggestive of positivity but he did not seem to have communicated that positivity to his face.

The man was still suffering the heartache of that breakup.

He had been in the odd, short -term relationship but he conceded that he was out of the habit of dating.

He did not have to tell me.

He must have imagined that he was talking about himself too much because he threw a rather, thoughtless question at me.

'Was Danny your first love?' he asked.

The mention of Danny's name gave rise to, the equivalent of a stabbing pain in my heart. I must have displayed signs of anguish as Andrew began on a profuse apology for his insensitivity.

It wasn't like Andrew to be so heedless.

He must have been kicking himself.

'I'm sorry but I got distracted with our talk on relationships'.

I sought to reassure him.

'No, it's not a problem. Bottling it up is the very worst thing, one can do or at least, that's what the psychologists say. Anyway, to answer your question, my husband wasn't my first love but I suppose, he was my first real love'.

Andrew wisely turned the conversation to the subject of my first love.

I did not have to think about that one.

'My first love was a lad who lived down the road from me'.

As I became lost in reflection, the past was being recreated in my mind and I was soon lost in my nostalgic reveries.

'John was the lad's name. He wore those round spectacles and smoked those roll-your-own cigarettes, and he wore his hair long and scruffy. I remember how he liked to see himself as an intellectual. He always seemed to be reading revolutionary socialist literature. Because of his love of the Marxist-Leninist theory, together with his resemblance to the great Beatle, the lads nicknamed him John Lenin.'

Andrew smiled at that.

Looking back now, I think that he was an intellectual and he did an awful lot of thinking about the world, unlike the rest of us, who were only interested in clothes and who might be on the next week's *Top of the Pops.*

The memories were flowing back into my mind, as if they were waiting in the wings, for their moment to reappear.

'John would tell us all about the revolution that was coming and how capitalism would be brought to a shuddering stop. I mean most of us did not have the slightest interest in current affairs. We could barely tell who the Mayor of Sligo was but John was well read on the revolutionary figures. He always wore that black *Che Guevara* T-shirt with great pride. I'm pretty sure he wore it to bed. Some people considered him to be a dangerous communist but he posed no threat to anyone. He was just an intelligent lad, who read a lot and probably enjoyed the notoriety of being different.'

Wow, I had got so carried away with my reflections that I lost track of where I was. I looked across the table at Andrew. Far from being bored, he seemed engrossed in what I had been saying or maybe he just indulging me. I felt rather embarrassed because I had droned on and on about a character I had not thought of for decades.

'Whatever became of that John bloke?' Andrew wondered. 'Did he join a kibbutz or emigrate to Cuba or what?'

That's what a lot of people would have predicted.

'He didn't do any of those things. The last I heard, he was working, as an estate agent in England'.

Andrew smiled.

' You know, strange as it may seem, I was a bit of a leftie myself'.

You could have knocked me down with a feather.

Andrew, to me, was the epitome of sedate, middle-class conservatism. What a difference a few years can make!

'That wasn't today or yesterday.' I declared.

He laughed at my unintentional bluntness.

'Yea, in my twenties, I was in the *Young Socialist* movement and believe it or not, Ms Keane, the man sitting opposite you once stood for the local elections under the *Young Socialist* banner'.

He was certainly full of surprises. You certainly can't judge a book by the cover.

' And how did you get on?'

He laughed again. It was a natural and unselfconscious laugh, quite the most natural thing I had ever heard from him.

'I received a ringing endorsement from eighty-four of my constituents'.

I wondered whether he had that little goatee.

' A hairy chin! Oh yes! Everyone had to have one of those. Even the women had to have one', he joked.

'I would love to see those photos but tell me Andrew, when did you ditch that socialism stuff?'

That question seemed to genuinely surprise him.

'What makes you think I ditched it?' he asked.

I pointed to the labels he was wearing.

'With those designer labels, you don't exactly fit the bill for a socialist, not even of the smoked-salmon variety'.

He took my point with good humour.

'Nothing is too good for the workers!' He retorted.

That was a good reply.

'Lucy, middle age is defined as the time, when the broad mind and the narrow waist change places. I suppose that is what happened with me too'.

As time moved towards eight o'clock, Andrew told me that he had a table booked for us upstairs in the restaurant.

'Just a little bite to eat! Nothing fancy! They are really good here'.

The restaurant was quite full. Alongside of us was, what seemed like a family grouping of five people and behind them again, was a young lady sitting unselfconsciously at a table for one. She was so incredibly brave, I thought.

The drink was beginning to loosen me up also. I surprised myself by telling him that my best friend, Karen was going out the following night with a man she had met on a dating site.

'That is fascinating. Let me know how things go'.

Maybe he was contemplating a similar strategy.

I promised that I would keep him informed.

'Does she know anything about this bloke in advance?' he queried.

'Well, very little really! She has a picture of him and he had one of her. All she knows is that he is a primary school teacher and he is interested in sport and books. That's the sum total of it'.

'She must have liked his profile picture?' he figured.

'She didn't really. I saw the picture. He is no oil painting but Karen is not a shallow person. She will give him a chance to show that he is a kind and decent sort.'

Andrew seemed relieved.

'Well, I suppose, with people like your friend around, it gives us all a bit of a chance'.

I didn't feel that he was fishing for compliments but I did tell him that his looks would not deter any woman. It was certainly faint praise but he accepted it nonetheless.

We chatted very freely about living alone, about coping with loss and interestingly enough about music. We discovered that both of us were Bruce Springsteen fans.

'Imagine you loving *The Boss'*, he said.

'Yea, I'm talking about the singer', I clarified.

He smiled but neither of us was keen on going down that road.

The time flew. That is always a good sign. I have to confess that after the initial awkwardness, I felt very much at ease with Andrew. I certainly got a glimpse of the man behind the managerial mask. Surprisingly, he was particularly good company. We were similar in one respect at least. We were both lonely and often sad figures, doing our best to live out our lives, while coping with ghosts from the past.

We chatted away until we were the last diners in the room. The taxi dropped me home first and as I was about to leave the car, he leaned forward to plant a little peck on my left cheek. I'm sure that he was just being gentlemanly.

Back home, I opened my front door and entered my code to disarm the security system. Once inside, I removed my high heels, placed my earrings and mobile phone on the hall- table before walking to the living room, where I plopped down on an armchair.

I sat still and replayed the events of the night over and over in my mind.

I smiled as I recalled some of the highlights of the evening.

Then, almost instantly my mood changed. A feeling of great guilt suddenly overwhelmed me.

I had done something dreadful.

My Danny was dead and I had been out enjoying myself.

I was a terrible widow.

Chapter 21

I was waiting to meet my on-line date in *Bewley's Oriental Cafe* on Grafton Street. I was nervous, as it was my first meeting with anyone under my new identity. I wanted to make a good impression on her. I knew that she would be my best conduit to Lucy. In my previous incarnation, I had seen Karen as a pest, who was encroaching on my time with Lucy. In retrospect, I can see that she had been a better friend to Lucy than I ever had been.

From my male standpoint, the notion of a woman needing a confidante was a difficult one. Karen, no doubt, had proved her worth as Lucy's V.B.F. Any resentment, which I might felt towards Karen had disappeared and now I fully appreciated that she was an amazing friend to Lucy. I knew also that Lucy needed Karen now, more than ever.

It was not about me anymore.

As this was a special date by any standards, I made a particular effort to be well groomed and fragrant. I was still unhappy with my new appearance but I had no choice but to make the best of a bad job. I was as weedy and as nerdy-looking an individual as I have ever seen. To add to my feelings of discomfort, my new job was far from what I would have chosen.

Thankfully, I had no preparation for my role as a teacher. I had been assured that it would come naturally to me. The same thing applied to my backstory for Karen. I knew that according to this pre-ordained plan, I was confident that she would be interested in starting a relationship. I was going to treat Karen like the lady she was. I owed her that much.

Karen strolled into the cafe a good five minutes ahead of schedule. I saw her enter and stood up to signal my position.

When she saw me, she smiled broadly. She would have recognised my face from my on-line picture. Thankfully, she did not seem deterred.

It was incredible to sit down with a girl, whom I had known for years even if I was looking at her through fresh eyes, in more ways than one.
She looked well.

The day outside was bright and sunny as the late summer temperatures soared. She was dressed in a sexy, figure-hugging pink blouse, with the top three buttons undone, creating a surprisingly attractive cleavage. Three-quarter length navy trousers dropped from a very attractive narrow waist and highlighted a glorious summer tan, which looked more real than fake. It must have been a better summer than some of the more recent ones, which I had experienced.

I suspected that her teeth had undergone a whitening treatment. Her hair had been recently blow-dried. And she was so wonderfully fragrant! She had made a good effort. She must be keen on me.
Women can certainly scrub up well. If I had met her in a pub, as a single man, I would have been interested and there would have been chemistry there. How did I miss this in the past?
It was because I had been blinded by my aversion to callers.

My words of greeting gave me a slight jolt, as it was the first time that I had heard my new voice. Back in the hotel with Tommie, I had been using my Danny voice but of course, that would not work anymore. I began to wonder where Tommie might be lurking. I hoped that he hadn't deserted me. I felt sure that I would need his help again.

Karen seemed rather nervous and I have to confess that I found that to be very appealing. Nervous giggling accompanied some polite enquiries as to how long I had been waiting and whether I was as nervous as she was. I told that I was nervous. This seemed to settle her. We discussed our jobs and she seemed genuinely interested in my being a primary school teacher.

'I think teaching is a real vocation and a good teacher leaves an impression that can last a lifetime'.

'And that goes for the bad ones, as well', I joked but she was having none of it. Teacher unions could do worse than employ her in a public relations role.

I am ashamed to admit that I got quite sucked into the notion of the first date and the thrill of the chase. It was like getting back on a bike, after a long lay off. The skill never deserts you.

I felt the need to turn on the charm.

'You look stunning', I told her.

I was not spoofing either.

'Why, thank you, kind sir! And you don't scrub up too badly yourself either'.

It was easier than I had anticipated. I was enjoying the fact that I seemed to be in good form in the banter department. If it had been a football match, I would have had a few early scores on the board. There was even that surge of blood in me that, under different circumstances, might speak of possible chemistry between us. A wonderfully fragrant and attractive, young lady, sitting inches from me and hanging on my every word!

That really appealed to my vanity. It is always flattering and reassuring to be considered attractive even if I had the face of a pathetic loser.

It soon became apparent that a busy coffee shop might not be the best setting for a first date. The noise level was very high and there was such movement around our table that it became more difficult to hear each other. All the advice stressed that a busy, public place was the best location to meet but this place was getting a bit too busy for comfort.

Karen wanted to know if I had previously dated anyone on-line. I told her that I was a real-life online dating virgin. Even that got a laugh out of her.

It was not her first time to date online. She had met two blokes last year but nothing had come from either. She had been tempted to give it up but her friend dissuaded her from quitting. I presumed that the friend she was referring to was Lucy. I felt that another compliment was due.

'I'm glad you didn't'. I remarked.

'Me too', she said, sweetly and nervously.

'For the previous few months, I was preoccupied with helping Lucy, a young widow, a friend of mine, who had been going through a rough time. It was she who encouraged me to go back to computer dating,'

'I'm sorry to hear of that'.

'Yea', she explained: 'Her husband, a man in his thirties, was killed in a road accident last February…. on Valentine's Day actually. The poor girl was devastated'.

Things were going better than I could have expected. I had been wondering how I could have brought the conversation around to the subject of her friend, without appearing dorkish.

'Wow, to lose the love of your life on Valentine's Day has a very cruel and ironic twist to it. Did they have any kids?'

'No, they did not have kids. I think she was anxious to get started on that but he was inclined to postpone things. It was tough for her. She lost interest in everything and I suppose the bottom line was that she missed him terribly out of her life.'

I nodded as sympathetically as I could manage to, without overdoing it.

'It's sad. Tell me, was she travelling in the car with him when the crash happened?' I enquired.

'No, she was away at a conference that day. She works in an advertising agency'.

'I see and is your friend coping any bit better now?'

Her answer both pleased and surprised me.

'Yea, I think that she has turned the corner. The funny thing was that after she visited the spot, where she had scattered his ashes, she seemed to get the strength to carry on. She reckoned that she sensed his presence there'.

To Karen, this was important stuff. To me it was incredible, mind-blowing.

To her, I must have looked bored and disengaged.

'Sorry, Jack, I did not intend to mention this on a first date. Sorry for bringing the mood down'.

I assured her that this was not the case but yet sensed her reluctance to continue with that topic of conversation. I decided on one last attempt to get up-to-date information on Lucy.

'Well, I hope your friend has brighter days ahead and who knows she too, might love again? '

I felt such a hypocrite.

'I certainly hope so. She has been out on a kind of date recently. There is this guy, called Andrew, who is her immediate boss. He has been showing an interest'.

Wow, it didn't take Andrew long to make his move. I saw him there with her at the hospital, probably worming his way into her affections. He was probably thrilled when I snuffed it. It cleared the way for him to make his move. He didn't wait very long.

I tried to hide my disgust.

'Her superior! That sounds a little awkward', I chanced.

I wanted to know if Lucy was playing ball with him or whether he was doing all the chasing.

'Has she any feelings for him?'

Karen was equivocal on that point.

'It's funny you should mention that! She saw him as being stiff and boring but seemingly he has lightened up quite a lot'.

I would have thought that he was stiffer than ever now.

My new face must be more expressive than my old one.

'You don't seem to approve', she remarked.

Apparently, I was letting my mask slip somewhat.

'No, it's not that. It's just that I think that her boss might be taking advantage'.

She agreed that such a fear might be well founded.

That marked the end of our discussion on Lucy for the moment but I was determined that I would get back on that topic on our next date, which I knew was already in the bag. No pressure!

We sat there for another hour or so laughing and talking about our hopes and dreams. She wanted only to love and be loved. It was no more complicated than that.

Chapter 22

I could not wait to see how Karen got on with this lad called
Jack. I hoped that he might prove to be her *Mr Right*. I had
asked her to give me a call and tell me how she had got on but I
did not expect to see her at my door, less than an hour after she
had left him.

She was more animated than I had seen her in a long time. The
words just poured out of her.

'It went well. He was so nice and unusually for fellows, he was
such a great listener.'

I asked the all-important question.

'Are you going to see him again?'

She was beaming with delight.

' Oh! Hopefully. He was so gentlemanly and yet so coy about it.
Near the end of our chat, he told me that he had really enjoyed
my company and very politely asked me for a second date.'

'And did you agree to the second date?'

'Of course I did! And what was great was that he made me feel
so relaxed. I was a bit nervous at the start but he admitted to
being nervous too and I think both of us relaxed after that.

'Do you know Lucy, it was his first time doing on-line dating
and he readily admitted that he had very little experience with
women? He is very funny without intending to be funny, like
when he said that he is a cyberspace virgin'.

'I wonder if he's a virgin in any other sense.' I ventured.

'I doubt it. He was much more relaxed than I was. I don't think
he's a novice where the women are concerned'.

I was delighted to see Karen all buzzing and so excited in her
girlie way. Her eyes were sparkling, something which they had

not been for a long time. There is nothing like a new man to get a woman going again.

'Oh, Lucy, you would love him. He is so intelligent, he can talk to a woman about anything, and he actually listens when you are talking. If he sticks around, I will engineer some way of getting you to meet up with him'.

'I would like that'.

The thought crossed my mind that Danny, in his day, would not have been favourably disposed to Jack. He had little time for men teachers, with their permanent jobs and long holidays.

Karen was able to recall every minute of their ninety-minute or so encounter. She may have been nervous but she was observant and focused.

'I told him that you had encouraged me to do the online dating and I filled him in on your loss and how you were coping with things. I hope you don't mind'.

'No, not at all! Why should I mind?'

I could well understand how my story might have a certain shock-value in conversation. Any conversational port in a storm, I imagined.

'I bet that killed the mood!'

Karen laughed. It had served its purpose.

'No, he seemed genuinely interested and he thought it was encouraging that you had starting socialising again'.

'I hope you didn't give him the impression that I was out pulling the fellows again. You realise, of course, that Andrew and I are not like that. We are just ..'

'Just good friends, as they all say', she teased.

I felt that I needed to clarify the matter.

'We are just keeping each other company'.

Karen smiled and pointing her finger jokingly at me as if she had caught me out.

'Oh, I see. Now it's company keeping, is it? We have moved up a level so'.

That is not what I meant and she knew it but I felt that I could be protesting a little too much, like the formidable Lady Macbeth. I contented myself with a remark to the effect that she could believe what she wanted but that we both knew where we stood.

However, that was not entirely the truth. I knew that all I wanted, as yet anyway, was companionship. I looked forward to the odd drink or meal out with Andrew but it was not anything like when I started going out with Danny. There was tremendous chemistry between the two of us. I tried to explain this to her.

'There is no spark with Andrew. Now, I like him and the more I see him, the more I like him but I do not feel physically attracted to him. Maybe that will change. I sincerely doubt it. Can you understand, Karen?'

She understood.

'Yea, I can get my head around that'.

Andrew could be charming, chatty, attentive and most of all considerate. In a different life, he could have been a soul mate and maybe even husband but placed alongside Danny, who was the love of my life then, Andrew would always fall short. I doubted if I could ever come to love the man. Maybe it was just because Danny had been deified in my mind since his untimely death and therefore no one else would ever be allowed to compete on his level.

Karen was already anticipating the next date. Jack had booked Saturday lunch in the award-winning *Chapter One* restaurant in

Parnell Square. Depending on how they felt, they might also take a spin in the countryside.

It certainly appeared that Jack was serious about impressing Karen and I was so pleased for her.

Jack would not be able to dine in such establishments very often on a teacher's salary but at least he was making the point that she mattered to him. Such attention could only do Karen some good. I hope that it works out with Jack. A setback with another man, at this stage, could result in serious issues of self-doubt. Karen deserves better. I hoped that *Chapter One* would be the opening chapter, in what might turn out to be a great love story.

Chapter 23

This teaching job is killing me out. By the time three o'clock comes around, I am knackered. The job looks so deceptively easy from the outside. It is so intensive and full on. The relentless classroom interactions, the constant questions and most of all, the bloody paperwork, all take their toll. I have to go to bed as soon as I get home in the evenings for a good lie down before I can venture out again. I had some preparation to do but I had the unique advantage of the relevant information is automatically available to me. I don't know how I would cope otherwise.

There are ten other teachers in the school, excluding the walking-principal. I had imagined that there might be great craic during the day with my colleagues but we were generally too busy for craic. Every teacher had a large class for the entire day and supervision duties on top of that. It did not leave much time for chatting during school hours. However, the single members of staff socialise after school. We have our craic then.

My accommodation is a one-bedroom apartment. It isn't pretty. It isn't modern either but it is convenient. There is satellite television there, yet there is no *Sky Sports*. It is disappointing but I am sure I will cope. There is a small canteen at school, where I grab a Panini for lunch.

In the evenings, I cook a bit for myself. It is never anything fancy, usually just one of my three meal repertoire- salmon, lasagne or chicken pasta -bake. I am not going to go hungry anyway, whatever about going mad with the monotony of it all.

On Saturday, I enjoyed quite a different food experience to my usual. I decided to treat Karen and make lunch a bit more memorable than the usual fare on offer in the city. I took her to a fancy restaurant, *Chapter One*. The place came highly recommended.

It was good but it wasn't cheap.

What I spent there would, ordinarily, feed me for a fortnight but this was a once-off treat. While a coffee shop was fine for a first date, I felt it was time to create a memorable impression by going to a classier joint. Women love that sort of thing.

From the moment we walked in the door, we were made to feel special. The folded linen, the tasty wine and the artistry on the plate, all contributed to making it a special event.

Karen looked great in a knee-length figure-hugging pink, sleeveless dress. I was my usual stylish Jack in a blue *Sixth Sense* shirt and a pair of dark navy chinos, which I had picked up at a good price in *TK Maxx*. I also slapped on the bit of *Armani Code*. I was beginning to get used of my new look but I still disliked it. It was, after all, just a means to an end. I found that the best way to cope with it was to avoid looking in the mirror as much as possible.

I did my usual moaning about how wearisome my working day had been. It was more for the conversation value than a real grouse. Actually, I found the job to be quite rewarding. The day was intense but it finished early.

I asked how her week had gone. I learned that there had been one or two changes in her office that week but the civil service was going on much the same as before. She had dealings with some awkward members of the public. Some had become abusive.

'They have this notion that we are paid big, fat salaries and sit around drinking tea all day', she lamented.

I had to confess to being one of those in my time. I was now being re-educated.

Karen had quite a good sense of humour, something which had come as a bit of a surprise to me. I suppose I never really listened to her before. There was no question but she was more relaxed than on our first date. I think that the magnificence of the establishment impressed her and I picked up valuable brownie points for booking it.

The beautiful weather had tempted many people outdoors in recent weeks but Karen had already established a pattern of exercise and healthy eating.

'Don't tell me that you are on a diet, with not a spare ounce on you?' I remarked.

'Not a diet, I'm just watching what I eat really. I can eat as many vegetables and fruit as I wish but I cut back on processed foods and confectionery.'

'So no dessert tonight then! I might be on my own when we get to that course' I speculated.

She was having none of that.

'I certainly am', she declared. 'The desserts are class here. Anyway, a girl is entitled to a treat now and then or life is not worth living'.

'True', I said. 'We will all be dead long enough'.

I should know.

'True, that's a very sensible way of looking at it. 'Carpe Diem', like Robin Williams said in that film. Tell me, Jack, do you inspire your students like that? They don't jump up on the classroom table and sing your praises, do they?' She enquired.

'Not so far anyway! Maybe next week', I answered.

At an adjacent table, a lady had her camera phone out for every course and she would upload the image. It seems such an effort and for what? And the poor old devil receiving it, might be stuck alone in a flat, making so with a lamb chop, or waiting to have a *Dominos* delivered.

I mentioned that to Karen as it provided me with an opening to get an update on Lucy.

'I take it; you don't feel the urge to send a picture of your medallions of beef to your friend. What's her name? Louise or was it Lucia?'

Karen was pleasantly surprised at my getting her friends name almost correct.

'Don't you have a good memory? Up to the front of the class! I am impressed that you have been listening to me. I must tell her that you remembered her name. She would like that'.

'Or kind of remembered it! Anyway, how is she keeping since?'

'Pretty well actually, everything considered. When I told her that you had booked this place, she was impressed, I can tell you. She reckons that you must have a touch of class'.

'It's too much class I have especially from Monday to Friday'.

Karen laughed.

'I like a man with a sense of humour. And Jack, what qualities do you look for in a woman?

I said that this was beginning to sound like an episode of *First Dates'*.

Karen loved to watch that programme.

That came as no surprise.

'I never miss it but getting back to my question, what do you personally look for in a woman?'

She was not an easy woman to side-track.

Questions like that killed me. I was now expecting to be asked about my favourite colour or my favourite film. I had no favourites in anything in that line. That was a very girlie thing to ask but then, it was a girl who was sitting opposite me.

I thought for a moment. I felt that my answer had to sound wholesome and proper.

I must have looked as if I had not taken her question seriously.

'Go on! Tell me. I'm serious. And don't say big breasts either'.

'I wasn't even thinking that'.

I lied.

'Come on Jack, you are a man of the world, what are the qualities that attract you to a woman?'

If she only knew that my Jack character had never been with a woman before or with anyone for that matter. He was fresh out of the bubble -wrap.

This question was not going to go away for me. I had to think for a little while longer.

'As you said yourself, I think a sense of humour is the first thing that attracts me. I also like a woman to have a mind of her own and not be said or led by anyone.'

I felt that this might go down well.

I think it did.

She was still looking at me, waiting for me to continue.

I had to do better.

'And I suppose, I like a woman to take pride in her appearance and present herself well'.

She nodded but seemed a bit surprised at that.

'I wonder if that is for your selfish reasons or the woman's self-image?' she asked.

'Selfishness entirely', I readily admitted.

She laughed

We continued to eat and chat. The conversation flowed even more freely than the wine, and that was saying something.

I really could get used to this.

Maybe in another life, I could return as a rich man or maybe as a gigolo for rich ladies.

Karen was keen to probe deeper into the nature of the man, who was her date for the night.

'You know, I have said before that Lucy Keane is my best friend. Do you have a best friend?' She asked.

This line of questioning made me feel very uneasy. It was shaping up to being more like an interview than a date.

I had barely time to make acquaintances, much less have a best friend. Politeness dictated that I should answer her question.

I was tempted to tell her about my great friend, who had been my constant companion, up until the vet had to put him to sleep.

That might just be seen as facetious and shallow.

I had to make up something on the hoof.

' Yea, in primary school, I had a best friend called Daniel. He was a big sporty type, who was picked first for all our schoolyard games. I was never great at anything but he would always get me on his team and I remember he would always keep a seat for me on the bus'.

Wow! I felt that I needed to give my brain a rest after that.

Evidently, I had not been pre-programmed for small talk.

'That was lovely but I think, as men grow up, they don't confide in each other as we girls do'.

I readily agreed with that. I felt that times were changing in that regard with all the recent talk of mental health and wellbeing.

'Yea, we need that friend. If I didn't have Lucy, I think I might burst if I did not have someone close to confide in'.

I sensed another opportunity to pump her for more information on Lucy.

'And does she tell you about her life, like how she might be getting along with her new bloke'?'

She nodded in the affirmative.

'Yea, she does'.

I waited for her to elaborate but she didn't.

I had to try again.

'So, is she getting any more serious about her new man?

After sipping from her glass and licking her lips, she gave a very considered response.

'She would never see him in that way. She says that they are more like social partners but I think they are getting to be more of an item. And who can blame her? She could do with a bit of male company. It would be good for her as long as there were no complications, of course.'

God help us. None of us wants complications.

Despite our best intentions of taking in a drive and a walk, the wine, the good company and bloated stomachs put paid to that. Plan B was to order another round of drinks and remain chatting, at our table.

We chatted about life, love, about our greatest fears.

Her greatest fear was to end up on her deathbed and regretting that she had been too cowardly to grab life's opportunities when they came along.

She had given this some thought.

'My greatest fear is that I might suffer some illness or be in some dreadful accident that might destroy my good looks' I said.

I meant it as a joke and was disappointed that she took it as a joke also.

She was not dating me for my looks.

After about an hour, we bid a farewell to our hosts and made our merry way onto the street. I walked Karen to the taxi rank and thanked her for her company. I was considering whether to kiss her on the cheek or perhaps, graduate to a light kiss on her lips.

Karen decided for me. After leaning in towards me, she held my head in her two hands, while she kissed me open-lipped in a slow and sensuous way.

It felt good, really good. It tasted like more.

'Thank you, Jack! I enjoyed lunch and chat. We must do it again. Next time, it will be my treat. Do you have any ideas as to where we might go?'

'Sure, Karen! Why don't you check if there is a Chapter 2 anywhere around here?'

Chapter 24

I had big news of my own but being the good friend, I had to listen to Karen's story of her date first. At least her story brought joy to her heart.

'He even remembered your name,' she enthused.

Karen was pleased with her second date.

'There is certainly nothing tight-fisted about him'.

That was a good sign. If he were mean now, it would be a bad omen for the future.

'You will have to meet him. I want you to meet him and give me your opinion'.

I half-heartedly offered to host some pre-drinks for them but Karen was not so sure if that was the way to go.

'I'll tell you what. Sometime soon, when I know where we are going in town, you can bump into us, accidentally on purpose, you know', she proposed.

I agreed to do that but I didn't feel right about being parachuted into their company. Yet, I didn't want to appear less than enthusiastic. If the relationship blossomed, I would see plenty of him and if it didn't there was little point meeting him at all. In that case, he would just be another 'might have been' for Karen.

'Jack likes women, who have pride in their appearance', she announced in all seriousness.

It was hardly an example of major breaking news.

'Oh does he now! I teased.

'You should be grand so.' I reckoned.

For a moment, Karen was lost again in her musings.

' I was just thinking, I must treat myself to a manicure and a facial before our next date'.

This was beginning to look a lot like the real thing.

I was happy for her.

Now, I felt it was time for me to deliver my breaking news.

'I finished with Andrew' I abruptly announced.

Karen looked all concerned.

'Why Lucy? What did you do that for?' she asked.

'I saw another side of him, a side which frightened and disgusted me. If I never see him again, it will be too soon.

Karen sat down alongside me and instinctively held my hand, to support me.

'Poor thing! What did he do, at all? Tell me everything'.

For the next few moments, the attractions of Jack Reilly were placed on the back burner of Karen's mind, while she listened to my tale of woe.

'The evening had started, with no indication of what was to come. We had been out for an early bird meal, in a new restaurant on the south side, whose name I forget. Things had been going quite well, at least in my opinion.

The problem was that I had foolishly come to see Andrew, as being something akin to the male equivalent of you. You know the confidant and true friend without any sexual overtones of course'.

Karen knew exactly what I meant.

'Well, I sure got that one badly wrong. At the end of the evening, he drove me home. He seemed quieter than usual and a little bit uneasy.

I imagined this was leading up to an: 'It's not you; it's me', moment.

I could not have been more wrong'.

I saw Karen's eyes widen in wonder.

'Don't tell me that he proposed to you'.

'Well, if he did, it wasn't marriage, he was proposing.
'He had been trying to build up the courage to pounce on me'.
Karen looked disgusted.
'The randy bastard lunged at me like a tomcat in an alleyway. Before I could say 'Down Rover,' his mouth was pressed hard against mine and his hand was mauling my left breast.'
'Jesus, Lucy! What did you do?'

'Well, for a moment I was paralysed by the shock of it all. Looking back, he may have seen that as consent. Anyway, he continued to grope my two breasts and then I felt him, move one hand down between my legs. In less than a minute, he had gone from gentleman to predator. This lecherous bastard kept coming for me. I was worried for my safety'.
'Wow! Lucy, that is so scary. He must be a bit of a *Jekyll and Hyde* character. I would be very worried too. But tell me, how did you get away from him or did you get away?' She asked the question, with an expression of sheer horror on her face.
'I shouted at him to stop. He didn't stop. I found it difficult to escape from his clutches in the close confines of the car, so I had little choice but to fight. I started to slap him, slap him hard. It was not nice but it was effective. I think he got an awful shock when I starting thumping him. He took his hands off me and moved his body away from mine'.
He looked confused and aggrieved as if he were the victim of an unprovoked assault.
'I thought this was consensual', he shouted.
'There is no need to attack me', he added.
'It was you, who attacked me', I roared.
'Now open that door this second and let me out', I demanded.
By now, his excitement had somewhat abated and I stepped out of the car.

There were no goodbyes or good nights from either of us.

I stepped out of the car and ran to the safety and security of my house. Karen, I had been such a fool', I sighed.

'It was not your fault. None of this was your fault', she insisted. Maybe it was not all his fault either.

Andrew had got the wrong impression of where he stood with me. In my mind, he was, as yet anyway, nothing more than a friend, if even that. He was probably more of a social companion, nothing more. I presumed that he had understood this.

My God, Danny wasn't more than seven months dead. How could any widow be put through this opportunistic attack? There was no way that I was ready to start dating again. Apart from disrespecting his memory with an over-hasty liaison, I was not ready for such a scenario.

I have often heard that red-blooded men find platonic relationships difficult. With that in mind, I see little prospect of having any friendship with a man unless and until I am ready to consider moving on with a new partner.

Karen had the joys of her second date knocked out of her by the account of my adventures with Randy Andy. I assured that mine was an exceptional occurrence.

She seemed to accept that.


After she departed, I sat down and poured a glass of wine for myself. Relating the tale to Karen had rekindled my anxieties. I needed to relax and let my tensions ease.

I blamed myself for the entire situation.

I still miss Danny in virtually every aspect of my life. Certainly, I miss him as regards the physical intimacy of our relationship but then again a woman can generally cope much better than a man can in that regard. I miss him much more than I ever thought I would miss him.

I miss him emptying the bins and having them out for Wednesday collection. I miss his being a captive audience and a sounding board for all my stories from work. I miss the heat in the bed at night and I even miss his toiletries in the bathroom even though I often complained about the space they were taking up.

I had not disposed of any of his clothes. All of the suits, sweaters, shirts and pants were all in his wardrobe exactly as he left in on February 14. I have never even opened the wardrobe door to look at them. I have heard of widows, who retain pyjamas -top or a T-shirt of their husbands to inhale his distinctive smell. That would do me no good at all. It is not his smell I wanted to retain. I wanted to retain his character, his personality, his companionship and I failed miserably to do that. Someday soon, I will open those wardrobe doors, clear the hangers and pile his clothes into some black bags to bring to a charity shop. But that day shows no sign of arriving, not just yet.

I took two sick days on the Thursday and Friday but knew that I would have to face Andrew in the office. I could run but I could not hide. I tried to put all thoughts of Andrew and the office out of my mind until Sunday night at least. I wondered whether Andrew had reported for work on Thursday morning. I felt sure that he did. I also felt sure that he would have noted my non-attendance and would probably have been relieved.

On Saturday evening, I did not feel like cooking so I ordered a pizza.

Twenty minutes later, the doorbell rang. Karl, the pizza deliveryman had come to know me well over recent months. He looked a bit concerned.

'Hey Lucy, I don't want to alarm you, but the bloke, who is parked across the street seems to have undue interest in you or your house. I was down this road a half hour ago and he was there. And he is still there, as if he's checking your place out'.
I was suddenly very worried.
'I think you should call the guards,' Karl advised
Sensing that his game was up, a man stepped out from the parked car and walked towards us.
Imagine my surprise when I discovered that it was Andrew.
He had been stalking me. Things were going from bad to worse.
My heart skipped a beat. I did not want to deal with this.
I was very glad to have Karl with me.
Andrew held his two hands up as in a gesture of surrender.
'I come in peace', he said rather bashfully.
I said nothing. No words seemed to be needed.
He seemed apologetic and penitent.
He wanted to explain.
'I was parked outside for a while, trying to build up the courage to knock on your door. Can I please talk to you for a few minutes?'
I wasn't keen on that but I imagined that this might help him draw a line under our relationship.
After all, he was my boss and I had to return to work again.
'No funny stuff!' I warned
'No funny stuff', he agreed, while finally lowering his hands.
 I signalled to the pizza man that everything was fine.

I was no longer felt afraid nor even slightly concerned. Andrew felt that he had made a fool of himself and had come to set things right.

I indicated to him to step inside.

Back in the kitchen, I boiled up the kettle.

I made tea for two.

I was tempted to offer him a cool beer from the fridge but I decided against that. He was driving and anyway, I feared the effect any alcohol might have on him. Tea it was and there was more than enough pizza for both of us.

It was all so awkward. He had decided to call, so I let him do the talking. He looked embarrassed and contrite, rather like a schoolboy, who had been caught bullying in the schoolyard.

'Look here, Lucy. I am deeply sorry and ashamed for disrespecting you. I let myself down and made a total fool of myself.'

I was relieved to see that he was taking it on the chin, like a man. He was not blaming me or claiming that he had misread the signals.

The man had come to apologise.

'I know that I have possibly destroyed our friendship with my thuggish and loutish behaviour, but I do hope that you will give me a second chance. I am not all bad, you know'.

I knew that he was not all bad, nor indeed half -bad. In fairness, he was a decent man. I also suspected that his motivation, in calling to my home, was as much work-related as personal. The last thing he wanted was to have a disgruntled underling or worse still an underling who might expose him as a sexual predator.

I decided to do the decent thing.

'Andrew, you have been very kind and supportive to me since the accident and I greatly appreciate it. However, I think it was a mistake on my part to accept your invitations to the odd drink or meals out. The reality is that I am not ready for any of that and maybe I never will be. In the light of that reality, I don't want to mislead you. I think that the only proper thing to do is to end it now. You deserve a good woman, one without the baggage that I have'.

He seemed to accept that but he still wanted to be friends with me.

That was never likely to happen.

Although he did not ask it, I suspected that he wanted certain assurances from me.

I readily gave him those assurances.

'Andrew, as far as I am concerned, this draws a line under the whole, sorry episode. I will not speak of it to anyone in the office or in any way impugn your character. You are a decent man, Andrew but you and I have no future'.

I spoke those words with all the firmness and finality that I could.

'Ok, Lucy, I am glad that you are so understanding and once again, please accept my sincerest apologies'.

'Good night, Andrew'.

Chapter 25

There are a few men in the staffroom, which makes for a bit of variety. Don't get me wrong now. I love female company. However it is nice to have male company some of the time. I have often sat at a table in the staffroom and failed to understand what they were talking about. It was definitely an education. I learned a lot of things. *Sudocrem* is the best thing since sliced bread for a baby's bottom. *Pampers* are quite expensive but you can get good value if you shop around and no house with young babies should be without *Calpol*. And when a busy woman has no time to wash her hair, there is great value to be got in a dry shampoo or even baby powder.

I particularly enjoy Peter Mc Gowan, the P.E teacher. He is some character. He divides his week between our school and another a few miles away. Apart from the odd chat in the schoolyard or in the gym, we have met up for a few pints. Peter also takes charge of training with the local Athletics club. I signed on as a member for the season if I last that long around here.

I felt that it would be a pleasant way to spend the evenings. Peter would get us to do some warm-up exercises and then take us for a short run. These runs would get progressively longer as we reached some degree of fitness. We would also be introduced to the weights room and the various exercise regimes. I found it a good way to forget about the stresses of the day. It was good for mind and body, even for a second body like mine.

Peter was a newly single man, having recently been through a divorce. He and his wife had been living apart for the previous five or six years, so the proceedings went uncontested.

He is, what might be described as a man's man and that is not necessarily a compliment. In my opinion, he did not seem to be very bothered about leaving the ruins of a failed marriage in his wake.

'Listen, Jack, we gave it a lash and it didn't work out. At least there were no kids involved. I feel that it's better to accept the situation and move on. There is no point in looking back, is there?'

He was already geared up for another foray into the dating game. He had opened a *Tinder* account and made no secret of it. He showed me a few lovely looking girls, who had been matched with him.

'You know, I think I'll play the field while I can. Life has a way of moving on and in three years, I'll be forty years of age. Imagine that'.

I had heard of stranger and more startling things in my life but I agreed that it was utterly incredible.

To be fair to him, he probably looked a few years younger, thanks to his fit, lean figure and a full head of black hair.

I decided to try out one of my girl friend's questions on him.

'Have you got a type, when it comes to a woman?' I asked.

He thought for a second or two.

'One with good eyes, good teeth, good tits and a good arse', he answered in total seriousness.

'What about her personality? Does it have to be good too?'

'Oh yes, personality is important too but only after the other boxes have been ticked.

Peter, I suspected was not husband material. On the school grapevine, I learned that he was not always faithful to his former wife. The man was a bachelor at heart. He was like a wild animal, which could never be successfully domesticated.

However, when he was out for a few drinks, he was such good company. Nothing was to be taken seriously.

He enquired how things were going with my girlfriend.

'Great, Karen is lovely and we get on well together'.

'Good stuff! You didn't waste any time there lad', he said.

'Yea, well, when a man sees what he likes, he'd be a fool not to go for it.

'How is she in the sack?' he cheekily asked.

'Well, I won't be giving her the sack, for the foreseeable future anyway'

He smiled and did not pursue that point.

'You know, women sometimes pretend that they are not that fond of doing the business but if you deny them in that department, they will be the first to complain. My advice to any man is to ride the arse off them. That way, you will have no regrets, no matter how things work out'.

He must have seen some logic to that but it was not my way. I had never even been to bed with Karen but she was already hinting at her interest in a bit of action.

Karen wanted me to go away on a romantic weekend with her. She had been to Carrick-on-Shannon on a hen-night and seemingly, she had a mighty time altogether. She had images of romantic moonlit cruises on the river, lovely meals in fine restaurants and beautiful hotel bedrooms. I also felt that she wanted to use the occasion to take our relationship to a more intimate level. Unlike Peter, I was a bit reticent about the whole intimacy thing. I had good reason to be so. I felt that in being intimate with her, I was somehow being unfaithful even adulterous. But of course, there was a horrible new reality for me. Danny, my old self was now deceased. He was not coming back to anyone. He was cremated and is no more. His wife is a widow who will soon be in the market for a new man if I can nudge her in the right direction.

I am Jack Reilly and I need to get my head around that fact.

I had dragged my feet for long enough.

I would agree to go to Carrick with Karen.

Chapter 26

I met Mr Gleeson, the solicitor again today. He wanted any other recent statements, which had come into my possession or were delivered to Danny's office address. I had asked Danny's employers to send any such material to him also.

Andrew is still giving me the wounded dog look and I feel sorry for him. I may have over-reacted but he had brazenly taken liberties with me. It would have been nice if he could have played by the rules. He was good company, we got on well together and who knows what might have happened in time? But he was too impetuous and too premature in his approach. I considered that it showed a lack of respect.

It was still just months since Danny's death. His clothes were still in the wardrobe. It was only last week that I found a pair of his socks. They were lodged under my bed. That knocked me back on my heels. In my naivety, I imagined it to be a sign from him, an indication from him that he was still with me. I just sat on the bed and held them close to my face. They were an unworn pair but they had been his socks. If only I could return to the day when he took those socks from the drawer. I put the socks back in the drawer and said a quiet prayer for him.

I pulled open his wardrobe door to have yet another look at his outfits. Each one held so many memories. I touched the short-sleeved, pink, silk shirt, which he wore during that sun holiday in Tenerife last summer. There was the smart navy blazer, which he wore on the yacht, which his boss Bernard had rented. There were so many outfits and so many memories.

I knew that there was no rational reason for me to keep these clothes. Common sense seemed to dictate that I needed to dispose of them if I wanted to move on. Danny was never going to wear any of them again. The garments were of good quality and many charity shops would be very glad to receive them. But could I get rid of them?

I was not too sure that I could.

I had Karen and her new boyfriend calling over for tea later in the week. I might ask their opinion on the matter.

For a long time, Karen had wanted me to meet the new man in her life she didn't want him to feel under scrutiny. A dinner might appear too formal and scare him off. Dropping in for a cup of tea before they went out on the town seemed more casual and less intimidating.

My first impression of Jack Reilly was quite a positive one. He had a very firm handshake, which I admire in people. He looked you straight in the eye as he spoke. This was another good sign. Danny had always admired those qualities.

Jack was exactly as Karen had described. Fair enough, he wasn't a looker but he compensated for this with excellent manners and no little charm.

He expressed his pleasure at making my acquaintance and complimented me on the house and surroundings.

In the past, I would have been sceptical about meeting someone online. Karen agreed that she had been a bit sceptical too, especially after a few dodgy encounters but she was so glad that she persevered.

Jack was a novice when it came to on-line introductions and he was very pleased that things had worked out so well.

'Yea, Lucy, I hit the jackpot with this lady.

Karen smiled contentedly. I was genuinely pleased for her. She had earned her place in the sun.

Things had changed a great deal since my courting days.

In my day, there were no online dating sites, no dating apps and no singles clubs. You just went down to the pub or the club and hoped to meet Mr Right.

Karen explained that she has female friends, who are on sites, where only the girl can make the first move.

'It is not like it had been in my parents time when the girls were lined up against one wall and the lads would bravely cross the floor to ask a girl to dance. And the might well refuse to dance with the bloke. That was so awkward on both sexes'.

Karen was right. That is exactly what happened.

'Yea, if I ever feel ready for another relationship, I think I would chance going on-line', I ventured.

Jack seemed intrigued by this comment of mine.

'What qualities would you be looking for in a prospective partner?'

'That's an easy one, Jack. I would want a decent bloke, who was kind and loving and would be there for me.'

That was not asking too much.

I had enough of dating for the time being. I was anxious to change the direction of the conversation, so I asked Jack about his job. He told me that he enjoyed his work. Somehow, I sensed a certain lack of conviction.

Karen, who was still on edge, was nervously following our exchanges. She was understandably hoping that Jack was coming across well.

She should have had no worries on that front. He was gracious and appreciative. I liked the fact that he listened attentively to me. He made me feel important and valued.

Jack was also quite a good conversationalist and much more importantly, he was a good listener. I was a stranger to him but he seemed genuinely interested in my life and could empathise with my grief. That alone, set him apart, in my book anyway.

Jack talked about the loss of his father and how his mum coped in the aftermath of his death.

'I remember my mother sank into a trough of depression. She 'took to the bed,' as they used to say in the country. She gave up on everything, even her bingo. It took a long time before she was able to move on with her life again.'

I decided to ask Jack about the sensitive issue of his father's clothes and how long it took for his mother to deal with it.

Jack had a look of horror in his eyes. It was as if I was talking about throwing out a living man's clothes.

'Mum left Dad's clothes where they were. She used to cry about them at the start but later she saw them as a nice reminder. In the end, she gave them to a local charity shop. He must have been dead for the guts of three years before they got them. I'd say the styles had gone out of fashion and come back again before she got rid of them'.

That was a different but interesting take on the whole situation.

I knew that I could never move on while I clung onto Danny's clothes.

'Apart from that, how did your mother cope with being a widow?' Karen asked.

'Not too bad, I suppose. She missed him a lot. Her friends recommended that she attend a bereavement course. She found that helpful. She got friendly with a widower there and they dated for a while but nothing ever came of it', he said, with a trace of relief in his tone.

'Would you have liked if she had married that guy or any other guy', I asked.

'Well, if we are being honest, none of us wants to see our parents with a new partner but if she wanted to, we would have had to put up with it. My mum wasn't interested. She used to say she was so lucky to have found one good man.

I was interested to hear that Jack's mum had gone down the road of counselling after her bereavement. I had dismissed it as being of no likely value to me. I never had been one to talk about my feelings to total strangers. I was beginning to wonder about the wisdom of that decision.

Karen asked Jack to tell me about the poor little student, who was desperately, looking for a kidney transplant.

There were no matches so far but they were attempting to trace his biological father, who did not even know of the little boy's existence.

I felt so sorry for this little chap, not alone because of his health issues but because he didn't know his dad.

'Jack, how come his father didn't know about him?' I asked.

'Well, from what I gather, his mum had only a brief fling with the boy's dad. Seemingly, the relationship fizzled out and they went their separate ways. The girl discovered she was pregnant after the breakup. She probably didn't want to resurrect a failed relationship.'

I thought this was amazing. People can be so different.

'So Jack, you are telling me that somewhere out there is a man, blissfully unaware of the fact that he is being hunted down for one of his kidneys, to donate to a son, that he never knew he had', I said in utter amazement.

Jack nodded that this was indeed the case.

I could not fathom this at all.

'Sure, that man could be married or anything. Can you imagine the shock he will get or the shock his wife will get? That would fairly rock their world'.

Karen felt that it would be very hard for his wife, to attach any blame to him because it was well before she had met him but I was not so sure.

'I think Karen, that most women would find a reason to be mad with the man in such a case. I think that I mightn't blame him but I certainly would make his bloody life a misery'.

'Good on you Lucy! Give him hell! Karen laughed.

Chapter 27

'Surreal', is too small a word to describe it.

It felt so strange to be sitting there alongside my widow.

I would have given anything to be able to identify myself but that was totally out of the question. This was the price I had to pay for getting a second chance to clean up the mess I had created.

My biggest regret in life was that I had dragged my feet so much, when it came to starting a family with Lucy. I was very selfish in my thoughts and plans. I should have understood how important a baby was to her. I am no longer in a position to father her child but I might just be able to influence her choice of mate. It would have to be a genuine and sincere man, who would put Lucy first. It had to be someone much better than I had been.

The very thought of someone making a baby with my wife was mind-blowing.

Most blokes are dead sound but some are not. There are a lot of chancers out there. Women can be attracted to these chancers, even smart women. Who knows? Lucy could fall for one of them.

It would be great if I could take on the role of the mature and sensible male in the background, who might just be able to manipulate things to bring about the right result.

If I were to manage that and have Alfie sorted, I think that I would die happier than I did on the first occasion.

Having tea with Lucy allowed me to raise certain points and put some thoughts into her head. The whole issue of my clothes made me feel a little better because it was an indication that I was not forgotten. She still cared about me. She still wanted reminders of me around her.

However, the more I thought about this, the more I understood just how selfish I was still being. It was all about me, about my ego and my standing in her affections. I was so pathetic. While she retained those assorted rags, she would still be bound to the past. While she was still bound to the past, she could never move on. I had been taught that same lesson myself.

I needed to help Lucy, not to hinder her.

I needed to be in her corner, as nobody cares as much about her as I do, not even Karen.

When the subject of Alfie came up, I saw Lucy was livid at the very thought of a husband, springing such a story on an unsuspecting wife. That certainly was an education for me.

I certainly would have been in for a torrid time if I had made my way home that evening. She would have killed me and used my guts for garters.

I might well have been dead either way.

In a way, she is probably better off not knowing about my fathering a child with another woman. I will do my best for that lad but does it need to concern Lucy? I don't think so.

I might be dead, but I was still vain enough, to cherish my reputation with her.

I had been considering how I might help the young lad financially, but I learned that Suzi and her new partner were quite wealthy. There would be no money worries on that score. Having said that, I will see what I can do.

Karen Doyle is a lovely girl and I have more respect for her with each passing day. The only one to eclipse her is Lucy. I don't know what the higher powers have in store for Karen and me but being with her is no punishment for me at all. I had grown to like her, respect her and look out for her.

I would soon have to tell her about my decision to assist Alfie in getting a functioning kidney. It will be difficult for her to get her head around that. It would be difficult for me, had the situations been reversed.

I hope that it might be seen merely as a noble and altruistic gesture on the part of a selfless teacher, in response to the urgent need of a student. Most likely, that is why the higher powers placed me in Alfie's school.

Each day, I marvel at how well the whole thing was set up.

Great minds are at work there.

The devil doesn't have a monopoly on wizardry.

I have not met Suzi since my reincarnation. I know that she has visited the school to update the principal and to thank staff and students. Monies had been collected for cards and presents for the little lad. I was away on an in-service when the principal brought her to the staffroom. I appreciated that meant the time was not yet right.

I felt like a man with a mission. No matter what anyone thought or no matter what the consequences might be, my top priority was to get my son back to good health. I still bitterly resented how Suzi had kept me out of the loop where my child was concerned. Only for his illness, I might never have known that I had a son.

I wondered, how long it might have been before he came looking for his father.

If I had lived, that knock on the door would certainly have driven a wedge between Lucy and me.

It may not have finished our marriage but it would have undermined our relationship.

Then again, he might well have grown up, believing that his father was not worth the search. He might view him as a waster, who had abandoned him.

There would have been no winners in either scenario.

Maybe there are worse things than dying.

Chapter 28

Karen was thrilled that she had tempted Jack to go away for a weekend. She didn't care about the destination but Carrick-on-Shannon seemed to be as good a place to visit as any. What appealed to her was the notion of having Jack all weekend. While she was glad that Jack seemed interested in her as a person, she craved physical intimacy as well.

She was all in a tizzy about what to wear and how to prepare for the weekend away. Poor old Karen had already had herself waxed and tanned. She even sought my advice on lingerie.

I was no expert.

She wasn't buying that.

'But you have been in bed over a thousand times with a man'.

'True, but it was always the same man and after a while, you become heedless about things like that. But my advice is to wear black. It will set off your tan nicely. Don't go for anything too skimpy. Leave a little to the imagination until the unveiling', I advised.

She seemed willing to go with this but she was so very nervous and insecure about her body.

'I think that I will die of embarrassment. I'm not exactly Miss Desirable, now am I?'

I tried to assure her that she was a fine specimen of a woman and that Jack was a lucky man to have her in his bed and his life.

'And remember, he will probably be as nervous as you are'.

She told me that she and Jack had never discussed previous partners.

'Well then, that's another reason why you should just relax and seize the moment'.

Karen was in danger of over-thinking it all.

Another great concern for Karen was how she would look on the following morning after.

'I will have to sneak into the bathroom before he wakes up and apply my makeup. I look an awful sight without it. And my hair stands up like a soldier standing to attention'.

I had to laugh.

'I bet it won't be the only thing standing to attention in that bedroom'.

It was rather vulgar but it helped ease the tension.

I had to tell her to stop when she went on about her stale breath in the morning.

'Ease up girl, ease up for heaven's sake. If you don't stop over-thinking it, you will ruin the weekend for both of you'.

She knew that she was being silly but she could not help it.

'I know, I am a terrible eejit, Lucy'.

'No, you are no eejit. All that concern shows that you are normal. Every woman has the same concerns and men too, I'm sure'

I prevailed on Karen to chill out with a cup of tea. We sat down at the kitchen table and had a good chinwag. She spoke of how things had improved for her, since this time last year.

Life had changed for both of us.

This time last year, I was happily married and going to bed each night with the love of my life. Karen was unattached. Now a year later she was heading to bed with a man and I was retiring to an empty bed.

Even though I tried to change the subject and help Karen to relax, her mind was preoccupied with thoughts of the weekend.

'Did you and Danny ever run out of things to say to each other when you would be together for a long time?'

Here we go again!

'Of course, we had moments when we had nothing to say to each other. A couple, at ease with each other, can sit together in silence for ages. Karen, don't panic about the odd gap in conversation or try to fill them with meaningless chitchat. Act natural and let things be! He is the man. The onus is on him to keep the conversation going rather than on you. Maybe you should take a drink or two to loosen up but be careful not to overdo it. You don't want him carrying you back to the hotel and you covered in puke. Do you?'

Karen seemed horrified.

'Lucy, you could have a point there. I better ease up on the drinking but I was planning on downing a few shorts to give me a bit of Dutch courage'.

She had her case almost packed. This was a mix of casually chic jeans and boots for daytime and a slinky, black, figure-hugging number for dinner on Saturday night.

'And don't bring too much makeup. Taking too much time with this will make any man cranky'.

This prompted a good laugh from her.

Almost every aspect of the weekend was a source of concern for her, yet she desperately wanted to proceed with it.

'Lucy, I'm nearly too embarrassed to even mention it but I'm a real novice in bed if you know what I mean and I wonder is there anything you can tell me about it', she asked rather coyly.

I told her not to overthink it but to simply get lost in the moment.

Watching my best friend turn into a gibbering idiot over a man, made me think that I was very lucky to have had seven good years with Danny. The dating game was a tough business and I was lucky to be out of it for that time. I thought that I could soon be that gibbering idiot if I were ever ready to look for a suitable partner again. I was still a young woman. It was three years or more before I would be forty years of age. I wanted a baby. I was sorry that I could never have Danny's baby but I still wanted to be a mother. My biological clock was ticking fast and sooner rather than later, I would have to get back into the dating game.

 I was not looking forward to it, not one little bit.

Chapter 29

I was very familiar with Carrick-on-Shannon. As a good
Leitrim man, I had made the annual pilgrimage there to see the
county team play in the championship. Invariably, it was a soul-
destroying experience but every so often Leitrim emerged with
a win. Victory was then so very sweet. It was a case of: the
longer the wait, the greater the pleasure.

We arrived in the picturesque, riverside town on a frosty
mid-November Friday evening and checked into the *Landmark
Hotel*, just opposite the marina and boardwalk.

Karen was looking really well with her hair freshly
washed and blow-dried. After checking in, we dumped our bags
before heading down to the bar for a bite to eat. The place was
bustling. There was a great buzz but we had some difficulty
getting a seat there. Normally I prefer to stand in bars but as we
intended to grab some food, we needed a seat. After some
moments, a waitress, with an English accent, indicated to us
that a table had become free.

I felt a little under-par and had to force myself to get into
a jovial mood. In my heart, I was still Danny Keane and so, I
was awkward being here with Karen. It did not seem proper to
me.

I could tell that she was up for a great weekend and who was I
to deny her that? I also knew that there would be an analysis of
every aspect of the weekend when she and Lucy would meet
up.

I would love to be a fly on the wall for that one.

I considered that anything accomplished on a Friday
evening would be a bonus, considering that we were late getting
into town. When we finished our meal in the bar, we walked

uptown. I held her hand in mine and she snuggled close to me. The air was crisp and frosty and the riverside lights highlighted the dark waters of the Shannon.

Karen wanted to go back to the same places where she had been on her friend's hen night. I let her lead the way. We looked into a couple of crowded bars. There was no doubt but this was a happening place. It was standing room only but there was a mighty atmosphere, generated by hoards of partying young people. I pushed my way through the crowd and bought vodka and tonic for Karen and a pint of lager for myself. With the loud music, it was difficult to conduct a conversation, without heads touching. I wasn't complaining. Her soft hair seductively touched my face and her enticing perfume filled my nostrils. It all added to the intimacy of the occasion.

We had two drinks there, before sampling another hostelry. The next one was a quieter pub, on the parallel street, with fewer of the young and trendy, out-of-town set. We managed to get a table in the corner alongside a middle-aged couple. The lady told us that they were from Kildare. They were in town for the weekend to celebrate their twenty-fifth wedding anniversary. They chose Carrick because their first-ever holiday together was on a river cruise on the Shannon and they had a memorable time in the town. Karen was seated next to the lady, who had introduced herself as Myra. She appeared to be quite tipsy. Her vocal cords had been well lubricated and she had plenty to say.

I found myself talking across the table to Myra's husband, Des. We talked a little about football and how busy the town was.

Karen, unfortunately, mentioned that it was our maiden voyage, as a couple.

Myra was very excited about this.

'Oh my God, wouldn't be marvellous, if you both, came back here in another twenty-five years, just like we are doing this weekend'.

Des joked that he and Myra might turn up too.

'If I get my Zimmer frame serviced in time and manage to get my hands on a load of Viagra, I will be there. And if I haven't Myra worn out by then, I will bring her along too. Sure, we will all have the free travel by then.'

I had imagined that Karen would be deeply offended by their bawdy banter but on the contrary, she seemed to be highly entertained by them. Maybe the vodka was kicking in for her. I have to admit that I found them to be a bit tedious and wished they would just go away and act their age.

We had to hear how they first met. It was in a pub on the quays in Dublin just after the St. Patrick's Day Parade.

Karen told that we had met on the Internet. I wish she hadn't.

Of course, that was unheard of in their day and it certainly stirred their curiosity.

Myra reckoned that she would not have the courage to meet a man, whom she had only communicated with on-line.

'I mean, he could be a rapist or a murderer or anything. Were you not afraid?'

Karen did her best to explain.

' Well, I suppose there is always some slight risk but they try to limit that. The first meeting should always be in a public place. Actually, we met in a very busy coffee shop, so if you are sensible, you can limit the risks'.

Even though Karen seemed to be interested in talking about how dating has changed, I was growing more impatient. We didn't come on a romantic weekend to be stuck with a couple of nostalgic strangers in a random bar.

At the first opportunity, I made our excuses and we left. As we emerged onto the street, Karen stumbled on an uneven pavement but I managed to grab her before she fell. That situation seemed to be highly amusing to her as she got an attack of the giggles. The effect of the vodka was plain to see. She was in great form.

On our walk back to the hotel, the cold air seemed to sober her up very quickly. As we made our way along the footpath, she again, snuggled in close to me. On reaching our hotel, Karen chose to ignore the busy bar. We headed straight up to our bedroom. While we were together on the town, I was able to relax and enjoy myself but having returned to the bedroom, my mood changed.

Feelings of guilt resurfaced. Despite the new reality, in my heart, I felt that I was still a married man and my wife was on her own in Dublin.

Being intimate with a woman, while being in that frame of mind was problematic. There was no way that Michael was coming out to play under such circumstances. It was only then I discovered, that she had also ordered a bottle of champagne and two glasses to be delivered to our room. More alcohol was the last thing I wanted.

Just as I was undressing, Karen excused herself and went into the bathroom.

'You chill there, with a glass of champagne and I will be out to you in a few minutes'.

I didn't want to be a wet blanket, on what was a landmark evening for her, in every sense of the word. I popped open the bottle and poured myself a glass of bubbly. I took one sip and threw myself down on the bed, wondering how to play this.

Just then I got a wallop on my right arm.

'Come on Danny! Move over in the bed there.'

I nearly collapsed from the shock. It was Tommie, my guide from the afterlife.

' Christ, Tommie what the hell do you think you are doing here? Don't tell me you are going to be spying on us when Karen comes out'.

Tommie was the epitome of calmness.

'Indeed, I am not. Watching amateurs perform never did it for me! Anyway, that's not in my remit and even if it was, sure there is nothing I haven't seen before'.

'Very funny! But seriously Tommie, what the hell am I going to do? All this stuff has thrown me completely'.

'Isn't that the reason that I am here with you now? I need to get you into the zone. The problem with you is that you are thinking and acting as if you are still Danny Keane.

Well, you are not Danny Keane and never will be again. Get it into your head, that you are a different man. You are Jack Reilly, a man with no past at all to fuck him up'.

I was a bit worried that Karen might hear me talking to someone and I mentioned this to Tommie.

'Devil a chance of that. She is going to be in there for at least for another eleven minutes. You know, for some reason, best known to God, she seems to like you and she wants to look her very best for you. That poor girl has been worrying and stressing about his evening and only wants to please you. And, then we have you, you fecking eejit, behaving as if you were being called upon to commit hari-kari. Get a grip lad! There is a fine bit of woman coming your way. Make the most of it for her sake' he said, clearly beginning to lose patience with me.

'But what about Lucy?' I asked.

145

Tommie took a sharp intake of breath.

'Fecking Lucy! That's all I hear from you. Look here, lad! Lucy's husband is dead and gone up in smoke and one thing is certain. He's not coming back. Remember, the whole reason you are doing this at all is to help Lucy. Otherwise, you would be stuck back in that bloody field in Dromahair'.

Suddenly, it began to make sense to me. I could feel my heart lighten.

'Ok, you are right, Tommie. I needed that talking to. But Tommie, get lost now because I hear the toilet flushing'.

'Right then, I'm off but you think your randy thoughts now lad and give her a big one for Lucy'.

As I undressed, Karen appeared from the bathroom, dressed seductively, in a shimmering black negligee. She sensuously, undid the belt to reveal a matching bra and skimpy knickers. In truth, she was a sight to behold.

She looked so good. I did not need any encouragement at all.

I stood up, walked towards her and gently eased the negligee from her shoulders. It fell silently onto the carpet. I slid my fingers over her shoulders and upper arms. Her skin felt so soft to my touch. She removed her bra and looked coyly in my direction.

I took her in my arms and gently lowered her down onto the bed. I lay astride her, and we kissed passionately, while our hands hungrily, explored each other's bodies.

Wow! This alone was worth coming back for.

Karen, to be fair to her, was in no way shy or awkward. She got into the game from the kick-off and we put both our bodies on the line. We were well into extra time before we had our energies spent. It was so wonderful.

I can't wait for the rematch.

Chapter 30

Karen was beside herself with excitement. She called over immediately after work on Monday evening. It was clear she had a great weekend.

'I take it that it went well', I said.

'You could say that', she answered, grinning from ear to ear.

I was thrilled that things worked out for her. She certainly deserved a break.

'Tell me everything', I insisted.

'Tell it, right from the beginning and leave nothing out'.

She sat herself down on the couch alongside me.

She had so much to report.

'Well, first of all, the sex was great. Not only did we make mad, passionate love on Friday and Saturday night, we even fitted in a matinee on Sunday morning. We got the hat trick, as Jack says.'

I was both pleased and indeed, a little jealous and wanted to hear more.

It is always the quiet ones who surprise you.

They were indeed strange times.

'I want to know all the salacious details. Come on girl.'

Karen sat back and took a breath.

'Well, first of all, I had a bellyful of vodka on Friday evening because I was so bloody nervous. Unfortunately, I got a bit tipsy and nearly toppled over on the footpath. Only that Jack grabbed me, my night might have been over before it started. Anyway, on the walk back to the hotel, I had already sobered up a bit in the frosty air'.

I had feared something like this.

' Karen, I warned you about drinking too much.'

'You certainly did but thankfully, there was nothing lost. When we got back to the hotel room, we had champagne chilling. While he sipped on the champagne, I nipped into the bathroom and dowsed myself in perfume and body lotion. I came out lovely and sexy, as you suggested.

It had the desired effect.

He just took me in his arms and what can I say, except that he steered me in the direction of heaven'.

'So the drink didn't do you any harm', I ventured.

'No, but any more and I could have been in trouble'.

I did not recognise this free-loving, jocose and relaxed Karen Doyle. She had gone to Leitrim as an uncertain and insecure girl but returned as a confident and assured woman. She was truly on Cloud 9. She had a lovely man in her life and they had wonderful sex together. Life sometimes throws you roses.

We also talked about the hotel, the dining experience and the drive down but Karen was focused on the bedroom experience.

'I never imagined that men's bodies could be as hairy as they are', she declared.

'Jack had hair everywhere and I mean- everywhere'.

I was amused at what surprised her.

She wondered whether Jack might be typical of men in general in this regard.

'They are all inclined to be a bit hairy'.

As a joke, I asked what part of her anatomy did Jack show most interest in.

I was surprised that she had taken the question seriously.

'Well, my ass got more attention but then again I have quite small breasts but he did give both a fair seeing to. Maybe he thought that they would get bigger the more he massaged them. I'm sure he covered every square inch of me but from my recollections, my ass got more than its share of attention.'

Karen seemed keen to compare notes.

Lucy, would you mind my asking: Was Danny an ass or breast man?'

It was so unlike her to mention him in that regard.

As soon as she had the question out, she recoiled in horror. In her enthusiasm, she felt that she had crossed a line.

Whatever thoughts were in her head, were on her lips within seconds.

I took no insult.

'Well, let's say that he was an equal opportunity groper'.

Karen had a follow-up query. She was certainly doing her research and I could not blame her for that

'And, you don't have to answer this if you don't want but I am interested to know. Do you mind telling me how many times might a man be able to put on a performance, if you get my drift?

I had got her drift.

This conversation was going in a direction, which I could never have anticipated. I was not entirely happy with it but Karen deserved my honest answer.

'Well, Ms Doyle, let's put it this way! The greater the novelty, the more frequent the performance, if *you* get my drift.'

She got my drift.

'Oh! So familiarity might lessen the sense of occasion'.

'Got it in one'.

Karen made a point of stressing that Jack had been very gentle and considerate with her.

It was good to know that. He seems to have treated her well and fair play to him for doing so.

I could see that she was lost in thought and I gave her a moment to return to me.

'A man's apparatus is amazing, isn't it?' She suddenly remarked.

I was reminded of what Danny once said.

'It's a bit like Aladdin's lamp. You give it a good rub. And hey presto, you are in for magical time'.

It was great that I was there for Karen, as she needed someone to confide in. It allowed her to get everything sorted in her mind.

She wondered whether men discuss such details with their friends.

'I mean, do you think Jack is chatting to a friend about the sex we had on our dirty weekend away?'

I doubted that very much

It was great to be dating and to enjoy a dirty weekend together.

There is still a pressure that comes with being at that stage of a relationship but I could not envisage myself going down that route.

'Could I cope with dating again'? I wondered.

I would be as nervous as a kitten about that first night together. If I were on the market again, I would have to get back in shape. Some laser treatment might be called for. I would also have to get my hair-colour touched up and invest in sexy lingerie. Being married brought a certain ease and relaxation to life. The pressure was largely lifted after one's market was made.

It is not easy being single.

Chapter 31

I was wrecked on Monday morning. Karen had me killed out and the drive back was very slow and tedious. Slow moving traffic always put me in a foul mood. Lucy used to try to calm me by switching to *Lyric FM* but that seldom worked.

With Karen however, I had to feign patience. I was still at the early stage of our relationship. I couldn't let myself down like that. It's funny how one's behaviour changes with increased familiarity. At the outset, you are desperate to make a good impression so you put on an act. Then, when you feel at home with the person, you can be yourself.

Karen was certainly raring to go. It was good for both of us. She had developed an appetite for sex and I had the full load, as they say. After Tommie's words of wisdom, I got stuck in and enjoyed myself. The girl is actually in great physical shape. Her body was like a new toy for me. I could have played with it all night and not got bored.

Back at work, Peter Mc Gowan enquired how the weekend had gone. I told him that she had me worn out; insatiable she was. He seemed pleased to hear that she had a good appetite in that department.
'You have to take it when it is on offer', he counselled.
' So, are you planning to stick with her or move?' He asked.
I was staying around. I could never flit from one woman to another, no matter what body I was in. I must be a one-woman man or at least one woman at a time.
'I think I will stick with her for a while anyway, Peter'.
'He nudged me on the forearm.
'Hey, we might arrange a foursome some night'.

For a moment, I imagined he was talking about a sexual romp but then he mentioned the new bistro.

Maybe he was talking about after the meal.

Peter had important news for me.

'By the way Jack, that little Alfie lad, you were telling me about, is dropping into school to see his classmates today. That's a good sign'.

This was incredible. Alfie was in the building. This was marvellous news. I had to force myself to appear casual and detached about it all.

Maybe I was fated to meet him today. I lost my composure for a moment and just walked off without excusing myself. I left Peter standing there. I wasn't too worried. He had often done the same thing to me.

Checking in to the staff room, I caught a glimpse of Suzi. This was the first time I had seen her since February and the first time seeing her as Jack Reilly, the teacher.

I introduced myself. She shook my hand firmly. Her face was friendly but it bore testimony to months of stress and anxiety. Her eyes looked dark and sad. Her hair was tied in a small ponytail. Evidently, she had neither the time nor the inclination to apply makeup. She seemed to have aged greatly since February. She was, what I imagined her much older sister might have looked like.

'I believe the little man himself is visiting us today'.

'He is indeed', she replied, looking around her to check where he was.

'Ah! Here he is now'.

I feared that I might fall out of my standings with excitement.

This little lad, who was walking towards me, was my own flesh and blood, yet he was forever destined to be a stranger to me.

152

He looked extremely frail and delicate.

I felt like reaching out to embrace him but I had to resist any such temptation. I wanted to spend time with him and assure him that all would be fine.

It would have been marvellous if he could know that his daddy loved him madly and he was coming to his rescue.

Alas, I could do none of those things.

I had to play the role of a random teacher.

I held out my hand.

'Hi, Alfie! My name is Jack. I'm a new teacher here but I have heard so much about you. You and your mum are both heroes', I added, with a nod towards Suzi.

I had many crazy moments both before and after my return but none more crazy or emotional than this. I felt an urge to do something dramatic. I wanted to cry, to bang the table or in some other way release the pent-up feelings that I carried inside me. I wanted to hurry things along for him, to spare him any further suffering and to set him on the road to recovery.

I would get the nudge from the higher powers when the time was right. Until then I had to just get on with things as best I could and focus on sorting out Lucy's life.

I had presumed that I was disguising my feelings pretty well, until I got a nudge from a colleague.

'Will you look at you, all welling up! And they say men are not emotional'.

Suzi smiled sweetly at me.

'Are you a dad yourself?' she asked.

I shook my head rather than utter the falsehood.

'But when I have a child, I hope he will be as brave and as great as Alfie'.

This compliment brought a smile to Alfie's face.

I was so pleased.

It was the first time I made my son smile.

I could not take my eyes of my boy.

I could see Danny Keane in him. He had the same hair, the Keane nose and the same dimple in the chin. I could never deny him and I would never have wanted to, no matter what the consequences were. Despite his condition, he had a smile on his face. He was looking around the staffroom, with the understandable curiosity of one, who is not ordinarily, permitted to walk through its doors.

Dialysis, according to his mother, was very time- consuming and boring for him. He so wanted to be back with his friends. They lived in the hope of the phone ringing, with the news of a possible donor.

His bag was permanently packed. They always had petrol in the car so they would be ready to travel to the hospital at a moment's notice.

I wished that the call could come today but at the earliest, it was many weeks away. That was such a pity.

Chapter 32

Christmas was on the horizon and the thought of it filled me with dread. As far as I was concerned, I had precious little to celebrate. One year ago, I was blithely sailing through life, confident that everything in life would remain sunny for me.
 It didn't.
Fate dealt me a very cruel hand.
Last December, I had a husband. I had a social partner. I had a happy home life and I held out the prospect of becoming a mother. Now, one year later, I was a widow, lonely, isolated and thoroughly miserable. I couldn't see anything to celebrate. The faster this mad season of happiness and goodwill passed, the better for me.

        Christmas decorations were up all over the office. The working day was less pressured. Tins of biscuits, bottles of wine and whiskey had made their way onto the various workstations, together with copious amounts of mince pies.
Younger staff members were excited about joining up with other companies' staff at a party night in the local hotel. At least, it would not be the case of looking at the same old faces, rather like a glorified morning break. There was the real prospect of new talent being on the horizon.
Needless to say, I wasn't going.

        My work colleagues had been good to me after Danny's passing. I received great support and understanding from all in my section. However, time moves on and people forget. Other tragedies replaced mine in people's thoughts. After a few months, I was treated the same as everyone else. I wouldn't want it any other way but it was difficult, experiencing the pain of loss and grief, while one's colleagues are in the mood for revelry.

My boss, Andrew, has always shown me understanding and perhaps some forbearance, right through the year. This even continued even after I sent him away with a flea in his ear. I have often regretted my reactions on that night.

I know that I was in the right and he was in the wrong but I could have handled the situation better.

Yesterday after work, Andrew asked me to drop into the office before going home. I wondered what he wanted to say to me, that he couldn't say at my desk. I hoped that he was not trying to coax me into going to the staff do. He would see an office party as being a great bonding exercise.

Andrew was sitting at his desk when I entered. Unusually for him, his tie was loosened. Unlike his underlings, he seemed to be working harder than ever.

He seemed pleased to see me.

'Ah Lucy, thanks for dropping in. Take a seat', he said, pointing to a chair, which was at a right angle to his desk.

I hear you are not going to the Christmas do and I can completely understand why. In your position, I would probably do the same thing'.

'I thought you might think that I was letting the side down by staying away, you know the whole team working and playing together'.

He smiled.

'Under normal circumstances, I would encourage you but these are not ordinary circumstances. Being at the hospital with you gave me an understanding of the enormity of what happened. I think you are great to be as strong as you are.'

'Appearances can be very deceptive.' I cautioned.

'Well, I still think you have done well'.

He went on to explain his purpose.

'I asked you here because I wanted to give you a small gift. I know that Christmas will be an endurance test for you, but I feel it should still be marked in some way.'

I'm not sure that I would agree with him there but I let it pass.

He reached back behind his swivel chair and presented me with a *Brown Thomas* bag.

'Just a little something', he added.

When he handed me the open bag, I could see that it contained a beautiful red, Yankee candle and a bottle of what I presumed to be expensive French red wine. There was also a card, which I presumed to be a Christmas card.

'Thank you, Andrew! I appreciate the gifts and the card but I won't be sending any cards this year'.

'That is not a Christmas card', he said, by way of clarification. 'I didn't think it would be appropriate.'

I opened the unsealed envelope. On closer inspection, I saw that it was, a mass bouquet *'for the intentions of Lucy Keane'*.

It was a thoughtful gift.

'I'm afraid that I have nothing for you, Andrew'.

He flung open his arms in a dismissive gesture.

He asked me about my plans for Christmas. I told him that I was going to spend a few days with my brother in Sligo but I had no such arrangement made. My brother had invited me but I had not made any decision on it.

'Well, knowing you, I'm sure you will make the most of it.

Out of politeness, I enquired about his plans for Christmas.

He was going to his sister's place in Galway.

'Yes, she has young kids, you know, all looking forward to Santa. You get the real Christmas feeling there. I have to say that I will be glad of the break from this place for a week or so'.
I stood to leave and once again thanked him for his kindness.
'Not at all Lucy and remember I am always here for you if you ever need someone to talk to. And almost by an afterthought, he added:
'And absolutely no strings attached'.
That was good to know.

Karen insisted that I put up some decorations around the house. I resisted strongly. We came to a compromise. There would be no big tree with bright, twinkling lights in the hallway but there would be a small crib on the hall table. That was as much as I could stretch to. I did not want to feel like a total hypocrite.
She was at a loss, as to what to get Jack for Christmas. She was pretty sure that he was getting jewellery for her, as he had made a few enquiries, about her preferences in that area. She didn't know whether she should buy him a personal gift like aftershave or clothes or go for something less personal, like a voucher for some man's shop. As a teacher, she assumed that he would be interested in books. She wanted advice on the matter.
'With a bit of luck, Karen there will be loads of occasions in the future for personal items but maybe it's better, at the start to keep it simple and uncomplicated. Aftershave can be a very individual taste. I would go with a voucher for a smart menswear shop'.
My mind turned to what I might have bought for Danny this Christmas if he were still with me. I'd probably have bought him more of his favourite after-shave or a smart pair of chinos and a stylish shirt. He would probably have bought me more

diamonds. I love diamonds and he knew that I loved them. It made life easy for him. I have a drawer full of pieces of jewellery, from past occasions.

They say that diamonds are a girl's best -friend.

Well, they got that one wrong too.

After Karen departed, the doorbell rang but I ignored it.

Carol singers were out but I could not take any more of the good cheer. I had the blinds down, but they probably had seen my shadow in the house.

The doorbell sounded again. They were certainly a determined outfit. Maybe I need a Scrooge-like notice on the door.

'No junk mail or carol singers please'.

When the doorbell sounded for the third time, I felt that it might not be carol singers after all.

I looked out a side window and saw a courier's van outside.

I ran to the door, apologising for my delay, in answering.

I told him that I had a loud food mixer on.

'Sorry to disturb you but I have a package here for a Lucy Keane'.

'I'm Lucy'. I answered.

'Sign here please Mam....'

I made my scrawl on the electronic terminal.

'That's lovely and a happy Christmas to you and yours', he added cheerfully.

I returned the good wishes.

'What the hell is this about?' I asked myself.

I tore open the package. It was from my sister Kate. There were several items there but there was an envelope with '*Open this last*' written on it. This was typical of her.

I did as instructed. I ripped the packing on the item. It was brilliant. She had sent me a box set of the British police drama *Lewis*.

In the parcel also, were some delicious macaroons as well as a bottle of my favourite wine *Sancerre*.

I then opened the mystery envelope. She had included a letter. There was another piece of paper, which I left aside for the moment.

I started to read the letter.

*You can enjoy the box set when you get back home. Treat yourself to the wine and eats right away. Go on! Spoil yourself! The real present is more for us than for you. It is the pleasure of your company at Christmas.*

*Trevor and the girls are looking forward to seeing you. Enclosed find your flight details and boarding pass. I know that you prefer an aisle seat. We will meet you at the airport. And in case you are wondering, Mark knows and is pleased for you. See you soon, Sis.*

*Love Kate XXX.*

I checked the boarding pass. I was flying out on December 23. Kate was so good. Despite my reservations, I could not insult her by refusing especially as she had already paid for the flight. It looked like I was spending Christmas out of the country.

Maybe Christmas still had something to recommend it.

Chapter 33

With a bit of time on my hands, I surfed the web to research what was involved in becoming a kidney donor. I discovered that volunteer donors are generally close-family members. However, that does not mean that a stranger cannot be a match. There are sometimes high profile examples of this.

There are a few requirements. I must be over twenty-one years of age. That was not going to be a problem. I could be whatever age I liked.

I was sufficiently healthy unless Karen had me worn out. Most importantly, there must be blood-group compatibility as well as tissue compatibility. The closer the match, the better the prospects for a successful result. And there is this business of not having antibodies, which I don't understand at all. It all sounded so very complicated for an ordinary bloke like me.

As the wiser powers were involved, I was confident that I could successfully clear any hurdles placed in front of me but I had been warned that there were no guarantees.

My old kidneys were unsuitable because of damage sustained in the car crash but I again presumed that I would not be here at all if I were not a match.

In the lead-up to Christmas, there were the usual health warnings in the media, about drinking and driving, about the need to give blood.

On television also, there was a timely feature on a Gaelic football pundit, who had donated a kidney to a mere acquaintance. It was my hope that when the time came for me to make my grand gesture, people would presume that I got my inspiration from that feature.

Lucy, I discovered, planned on spending Christmas, in London with her sister. I hope that she has a good time there. This time last year, she was absorbed in the festive scene but I would imagine, that like me, she couldn't wait for the festivities to be over. Poor, poor Lucy! My heart goes out to her.

I am still riddled with guilt for my own part in my demise.

I have met very few people, who are as excited about Christmas as Karen is. She is a big child at heart. I think that being in a relationship means so much to her. I wanted to hand over my presents, while we were on our way back from the pub but she would not hear of it. We had to perform a simultaneous exchange.

Lucy could always tell what I bought for her. She would open the box, ooh and aah about how lovely it was, try it out and then ask me if I had a gift receipt. That probably said more about my lack of imagination than anything else.

She and I were a team, or at least, I thought so. We knew each other's ways and even though I could be an insensitive bastard, we worked well as a couple. Last Christmas Eve we were sitting around in our Christmas jumpers and sipping mulled wine. How circumstances have changed.

Not for one moment, did I imagine or consider, that this would come to such an abrupt end.

Before Karen headed down the country, I took her out for a drink on December 23. The pubs were all packed tight and there was a happy and good-natured atmosphere on the streets and in the bars. I don't think I ever really appreciated how much the season had to offer. Like a lot of other things, I took it for granted.

Karen got a little bit misty-eyed and told me that the highlight of the year for her, was when she met me.

Poor girl!

It was an enormous compliment but I could not help feeling sorry for her. She deserved better than a man, who was still in love with his widow.

Maybe it was just vanity on my part but I was sure that I looked a lot better as Danny Keane than I do as Jack Reilly. Yet, back then, she barely gave me the time of day.

Was it my undisguised contempt towards her or was I then, not in the frame, because I was a married man? The whole issue of attraction is a great source of fascination for me.

'Karen, I was thinking there of your friend Lucy missing her man at Christmas. It must be tough on her. What sort of a bloke was her husband anyway?'

Karen took a moment to consider. It was as if his appearance could have momentarily slipped her mind.

She looked around the bar as if struggling to remember.

'Let me see now. He was all right, I suppose but I always got vibes from him that he did not like me. He barely tolerated me around the place. Lucy used to tell me to pass no heed because he was just a grumpy so and so. Now, I know that he loved Lucy but he wasn't a man I could warm to'.

This was a sobering verdict.

I was no Mr Popular. I was seen as a grouch. It was not how I wanted to be remembered. It was too late to do anything about that now. That ship had sailed or more correctly, that car had crashed.

'He was nothing like me so', I ventured.

'Not like you at all', she said categorically

'Was he a good looking man, I mean, good looking, from your woman's point of view?'

Karen thought for a moment.

163

'No, he was nothing to write home about. He was quite tall and well built he was not especially good looking. He was very opinionated and if you didn't agree with him, it was you who was in the wrong. I'm sure that at times, he wasn't easy to live with but....'

I stopped her there. I had heard enough.

I was deluded perhaps about how Lucy and I got on together as a couple. I wanted to leave that conversation with at least some of my dignity and self-respect intact.

'Sorry Karen, I just remembered I have to return a call now. Just sit tight there. Hold my drink and I will be back in a minute'

I just had to cut her off. It did not make for easy listening.

I went outside to the smoking area. I didn't want to smoke. I just wanted to think.

I put my phone up to my ear and pretended to be on my phone, so that those around me would not feel that I was listening to their conversations. I was actually mulling over what Karen had said.

The penny had finally dropped for me.

Danny Keane was not a very likeable character.

That was a hard thing to get my head around.

I had always been a bit irritable and dismissive of people. I was also intolerant of anyone or anything, that didn't appeal to me. Danny's reputation was beyond repair.

Then, to my great embarrassment, my phone began to ring. I felt such a Wally. Everyone around me could see that I was just posing with my phone.

I must have turned puce from embarrassment.

I apologised profusely to Karen for abandoning her but she wasn't bothered.

164

I headed back to the flat. Karen was getting more and more philosophical about life and life choices.

'It's hard to believe that there is a pattern to it all. I mean, on this night last year, we were alone and single and not knowing that time was drawing us closer together. Isn't it all so wonderful, so seemingly random but so amazing?' She enthused.

We adjourned to her bedroom where I unwrapped myself and gave her the final part of her Christmas present. She really enjoyed it.

Whoever said that there is more enjoyment in giving than in receiving, certainly had a point.

Chapter 34

Christmas in London, with my sister and her family, was a splendid experience. I was treated royally and was never allowed to lift a finger. It was great to be in a house with very young children, who were so excited at the prospect of Santa calling. It brought back really special memories for me. My two nieces reminded me so much of myself, as a kid. I would love to have children someday and be part of that magic all over again. I was delighted to help them write letters to the North Pole, and get their stockings ready for Christmas Eve.

In the future, I want to celebrate a family Christmas as Kate and Trevor do. They were all there together and the feeling of familial love was palpable, yet understated. On occasions, I felt like an intruder but I can honestly say that it was all in my head. It was just my over-thinking of my situation.

Nevertheless, I was determined to get out of there early and leave them to their family holiday and so despite Kate's protestations, I booked my return flight for December 28. Trevor pushed me to see the New Year in with them but I was not for turning.

When I arrived back in Dublin, I did not detect the usual musty smell from the house, which I normally get, after it is locked up for a few days, especially in the wintertime. On the contrary, the house was spring fresh, as if the breeze had been blowing through it. This was a pleasant surprise for me.

I still almost expect Danny to walk through the door one day. I miss his company. I miss any company.

Looking at the same four walls, day in and day out, takes it out of a person. I knew that my friends were all with their families. There were no missed calls on my phone.

Nobody had been in touch.

After Danny died, I made a pact with myself never to drink on my own in the house. I feared that I might use alcohol as a crutch and that this crutch could well become the undoing of me. I took a drink when I was highly stressed, after being attacked by Andrew but I saw that as being for medicinal purposes, so I don't count that.

I reckoned that tonight, I was entitled to another drink. It was still Christmas after all.

On the drink's sideboard, in the living room, still sat the French red, which Andrew had given me. Now, seemed as good a time to sample it. I located the corkscrew and eased the cork out. The bouquet was tempting and it looked a beautiful full-blooded red. I poured a small glass and curled up on the armchair. It tasted of the warm south of France and reminded me of the summer holidays, which Danny and I had enjoyed. It was ironic that a gift from another man should remind me of Danny.

I began to think of Andrew and wondered what he was doing now. He had told me that he was going to his sister's for Christmas Day. The two of us had much in common. We were in the same business, worked in the same office, had both great disappointments in our lives and both were experiencing loneliness. I wondered whether Andrew was making resolutions for the year ahead.

Apart from one aberration, he had consistently improved in my estimation over the year. He had progressed from being the cold fish of the office to be a genuinely caring and sensitive creature. He was interested in me. I liked him but I could never grow to love him.

Maybe the fact that he was so different from Danny militated against him. Maybe he was not the type that I was likely to be attracted to. Danny was swashbuckling at times, insensitive very often, pig-headed and selfish also but there was undeniable chemistry between us. We had been made for each other.

I emptied my glass and when I refilled it, I raised it in a toast to Danny.

*'Here's, to you Danny Boy. I hope you are at peace. I miss you dearly but I cannot just die after you. If you have any pull or influence with the top man, up there ask Him to give me strength in the New Year. Cheers and if you have a New Year in eternity, I hope it is a great one for you'.*
Love you.

I then began to consider what resolutions I should make for the year ahead.
I decided that I would constantly remind myself that I was still in the land of the living and that I was a relatively young woman. I would not allow myself to go to seed. I also vowed that I would go out more. I should be involved in something, whether that be in professional development, having a meal with a friend, taking fitness classes; anything that got me away from being stuck in front of the television.
I resolved to make a supreme effort to banish negative thoughts from my mind and to stop feeling sorry for myself. Nature had dealt me a particular hand and I had no choice but to play it. I would play it to the very best of my ability.

I also set a deadline of mid-summer for clearing out Danny's clothes from the wardrobe. I also determined that I would be more open to the possibility of seeing other men.

Now, I certainly had no intention of throwing myself into the arms of the first available man who happened along. Rather, I would be open to the prospect of finding love again.

If it were I, who had passed on, I am sure that Danny would miss me enormously but I have no doubt that after a certain interval, he would move on with his life.

I felt I was entitled to one more tilt at happiness.

Once I had made my resolutions, I committed them to my little notebook. I dated them and I signed it.

That made it all official.

Chapter 35

I opted to stay in my old house over Christmas. Of course, Lucy wasn't there. She was in London. It was strange being back there but it was better than worse. I got an inkling of how lonely a place can be when one's loved one is gone from it. Poor Lucy must feel miserable there. I wanted to help her in some way but I hadn't a clue how to do so. I became clear to me that she needed a partner and down the road, she needed a baby to fulfil her.

I don't know why it was ordained that I should spend Christmas there. Maybe someone was trying to give me a taste of home life again. If so, it was a very poor substitute for the warm, companionable place I had known this house to be. Maybe I was intended to do something there or maybe see something there. The Lord certainly moves in mysterious ways.

I made myself useful when I could. I opened the windows to air the house. Lucy always hated the musty smell on return from a trip in winter. I replaced both the black and coloured cartridges in the printer. I also cleared out a paper jam. The lead on the connection from the satellite dish to the *Sky Q* box was a bit loose so I tightened that.

Her recent mail, which she had opened and read, was still lying on the table in the study. There was a reminder about a TV licence. There was also a bank statement as well as a couple of letters from people, hoping that she would have a good Christmas, despite her sad loss. They assured her that she was in their thoughts and prayers. There did not seem anything further than I could do so I just sat down on an armchair and relaxed in front of the television.

Very soon, I found myself being overwhelmed by sleep. In my slumber, I dreamed that I had been transported back in time to that fateful day of February 14. I was driving back to the office and I was wondering about telling Lucy what I had just heard. The big difference in the dream was that I had stopped at the red light. I rang Lucy to say that I was coming home early. Once home, I found myself telling her about what I had learned that morning.

I could see the tears well up in her eyes and then I could sense her rising anger. Just as I took a step back, she reached for the nearest thing she could get her hands on and flung it forcefully at me. I barely avoided being struck by the cereal bowl.

I dreamed that she was shouting at the top of her voice: 'I hate you. I hate you'.

'You disgust me, Danny Keane! You bloody well disgust me. You wouldn't give your wife a child but you could give that bitch a son. Get out before I do something I might be sorry for'.

The trauma of the moment woke me up suddenly. My heart was racing.

Thank God, it was just a nightmare.

I never imagined that I could be so glad that I was dead.

I left the house and walked and walked until I lost consciousness or maybe was put into a sort of idling mode.

The next time I saw Lucy was on January the fourth.

Karen and I were on our way to a dramatic production in town and she had invited Lucy along. It was part of an effort on Karen's part to get Lucy in circulation again and I certainly approved of that.

Lucy had insisted that we have some pre-theatre drinks in her place.

When she answered the door to us, she was smiling broadly and embraced both of us.

It felt so good to hold her again.

'I'm sorry Jack for playing gooseberry but your girlfriend is very persuasive. She tells me that she is my social secretary for the coming year'.

I was delighted to hear it

It was shades of the old Lucy.

When we reached the theatre, there was no stopping her from paying for the drinks in the foyer bar. I was never comfortable with a woman paying but I let it go on that occasion.

While we chatted about the weather and the crowd, Lucy was scanning the attendance, checking to see who was out and about. She seemed to be in such good form, that I suspected she was just painting a smile on her face while hurting inside.

As it happened, the play was eminently forgettable but none of us cared. It was little more than an excuse to be out. I recalled how Lucy always loved a special treat on the way home from the pub or the theatre. She was especially partial to a great, big, juicy burger and chips. Lucy adjudged it to be the highlight of the evening.

She was as giddy as a kid getting an unexpected treat.

Karen wasn't hungry. I shared my chips with her.

Looking at Lucy tucking in with relish, I could only smile.

'This is the life', she said, as she tucked into her favourite fast food.

Chapter 36

The night out with Karen and Jack was such a bittersweet night for me. I painted a smile on my face and hoped for the best. I was not going to jettison my resolutions in the first week of January. My mind was not on the staged drama. I was considering the drama of my own life.

In the foyer bar, I had a good look at the patrons, as they arrived for the performance. I imagined, what their circumstances might be. I wondered if any of them was in my position. I kept up a cheery front. I smiled on all that smiled at me.

I was tempted to decline Karen's invitation but she told me that she and I had our very own mutual support group. In the past, I had taken her out when she needed a companion, so she was reciprocating. The difference was that she was in the early stages of a new relationship, when a couple, typically prefer to stick together.

Jack was very good to agree to go along with her on this. He could have objected but he didn't. When he had an opportunity to put a natural end to the evening and drop me home, he opted to bring me for fast food. That was a blast from the past from me. The taste of that juicy burger made the evening for me. It was as if I had unearthed part of my self, which had been buried for months.

It set me thinking. When I got home, I luxuriated in a hot, fragrant bath. After I dried myself off and before I put on my night attire, I took a good look at myself in the full-length mirror. It was a sort of stocktaking exercise, I used to regularly work out but of course, this had gone by the wayside as well. I got a bit of a shock when I saw what was looking back at me.

Since my troubles started, I had taken to comfort eating. My clothes felt a little tight for me now. I stepped on the scales and discovered that, while I hadn't put on quite as much weight as I had feared, I was still carrying an extra nine pounds.

That extra poundage had to go.

I would have to get moving again and soon. Those running and exercise nights down at the local gymnasium seemed like a good fit for me.

I then sat down at my dressing table and studied my face and hair. There were strands of grey hair among the black, which had lingered unnoticed.

The hair itself looked limp and dull and the trademark sheen was sadly absent. Remedial action was called for. My combination skin was now predominantly dry and in places blotchy. I had been letting myself go. That would have to stop if I ever were to rescue the situation before it was too late.

Danny's anniversary was coming up next month and I wanted to have solid progress made before then. He would have been so disappointed if I were to let myself go. Even though I had an excuse for letting go, that was little comfort. There was a harsh reality for me to face and I needed to face it sooner rather than later.

I got a text from Karen asking to meet me after work. I suggested a coffee shop but she wanted to come over to my place. I wondered what was up with her.

When she arrived she was all in a fluster.

'Martin has been in touch with me again. Can you bloody believe it?'

Martin was a young accountant, who had broken Karen's heart, when he jilted her after several months of courtship. She was really into him. That episode had been a shattering blow to her confidence.

I shook my head disbelievingly.

'After all these years! I thought he was in London'.

'Well, he was but seemingly he's coming back to Dublin and he has got a job in the *Financial Services Centre'*.

I asked intrigued, as to why this heart-breaker should suddenly reappear after an interval of seven or eight years.

'Well, he contacted me just before I texted you last night'.

'Did he call or *Facebook* you or what?

'He rang me'. I hadn't changed my mobile number since we were dating'.

I felt that Martin was bad news and the last thing Karen needed now, when things had been going so well with Jack.

'What is he looking for now at this stage. Is he married or single or separated or what?'

I suddenly realised that I was asking more questions than a quiz show host.

I needed to stop badgering her.

'Single, well single now anyway'.

The only thing that she was certain of was that he wanted to meet up with her again.

'I was so shocked. I was hardly able to say anything to him at all'.

'And did you agree to meet him?'

'No, I didn't. I told him that I was in a relationship but he didn't seem bothered. He said that he would give me a bit of time to get my head around the situation'.

That sounded like the old Martin. He expected people to jump when he clicked his fingers.

Karen explained, that on a recent trip to Dublin, Martin had seen her profile on *Tinder*.

'You wouldn't consider getting back with him would you?' I asked, already fearing that she was setting herself up for another fall.

'Of course not', she answered.

Her tone was less than convincing.

'I thought he was the love of my life but he let me down so badly. Imagine telling me that I was the one for him and then carrying on behind my back with that Ellie, tramp. At least, in those innocent days, he never managed to tempt me to bed with him', she said with relief in her voice.

She showed me a screen shot of his profile picture.

Martin's looks had not dis-improved in the interim.

He looked the same old Martin but there was a less boyish and more mature look to him. Facially, he reminded me of that Aidan Turner guy from *Poldark*. He would beat Jack Reilly hands down in the looks department but Jack would wipe the floor with him, when it came to character and decency.

I feared that Jack was not sufficiently rooted in her affections, to withstand a full-scale onslaught from her former lover. It was going to be my job to make her see sense. I did not want to have to pick up the pieces after another disappointment for her.

'Yea, he is good looking all right but what does that count for?' I asked.

'But there never are any guarantees with any man', she rightly cautioned.

'You know the old line, Karen: 'Fool me once, shame on you. Fool me twice, shame on me'.

'You need not worry. I have told him that I have moved on'.

He was not going to buy that. If he did, more fool he.

'He will be back to you. He will sound as nice and as plausible as he possibly can. You will be reminded of all the good times, you enjoyed together and you might still feel some of those butterflies in your stomach. You have to be strong, Karen, really strong and send this guy packing'.

I asked whether she had researched anything on him. She had.

He was a high-flyer professionally but she could find no information at all about his personal life. That was eating her up.

I knew that, regardless of what she said, she would meet up with him again, even if just to satisfy that curiosity.

'Have you told Jack yet or are you going to tell him at all?'

She had no intention of telling him.

At least, that was one good call on her part.

Telling him might sour their relationship.

Karen turned to her *Tinder* profile picture and considered it carefully for a few moments.

'At least it was a good picture. I had lost the chubby cheeks, which I had for a few years'.

I asked Karen why she didn't alert me to my weight gain. 'I didn't because it was inevitable, in the short term at least. If I were in your position, I'm not sure I would get a house door big enough for me to get through', she replied.

'But you are taking the first steps to get back to your old self', she said encouragingly.

I told her that I thought her Jack was great to let me join them on their night out. She said that he enjoyed my company and often enquired about me. He proposed doing a threesome again soon.'

'That was an unfortunate choice of words for you girl', I said.

'Can you imagine if someone else overheard that comment? I don't think an innocent night at the theatre is what would come to mind.'

Karen laughed nervously.

'Maybe it was a Freudian slip on your part, Karen. I mean, you with two rival lovers chasing you'.

'Yea', she added. 'My mother used to say men are like buses, you wait a long time for one and then two come along together'.

Chapter 37

Karen had come off the phone and she looked a bit flustered.
'Is everything all right, Karen?' I asked.
She assured me that it was.
I had decided that it was time to tell her about my intention of becoming a living donor for Alfie if I were deemed suitable.
She looked a bit distracted and I am not sure that the full impact of what I was saying had registered with her.
'That has to be a long shot,' she commented.
She was still very puzzled or maybe just a little preoccupied.
'Have you mentioned this to the lad's family?' she asked.
' I wanted to tell you first.'
Her reaction came as a bit of a surprise to me. I didn't know what sort of response I was expecting. I felt that I might well have got a similar reaction if I had told her that I intended to give a hundred euro to the Kidney Association of Ireland.
        I was sure that the powers above would somehow, arrange for me to bump into Suzi. That is exactly what happened. Our cars had been parked alongside each other in *Jervis Street Centre* car park. I was closing the boot of my car when I saw her coming in my direction.
She smiled at me as she may have smiled at anyone in the same position.
She may have recognised me as being vaguely familiar. In any case, I greeted her and re-introduced myself as Jack Reilly, a teacher at Alfie's school.
She smiled.
I reminded her that we had met once before. She acted as if she had remembered but somehow, I doubted it.
I asked how the young man was.

'He's not bad at the moment but it is very limiting on him. I can't see him being back at school this year anyway'.

I also told her about my interest in becoming a living donor, ever since that television programme.

Suzi's reaction was not dissimilar to that of Karen when I told her of my offer. It was wonderful that a man was being so noble and altruistic in his thoughts but I felt that she didn't take my offer seriously.

'It's a long, long shot, Mr Reilly but I am so appreciative of you for putting yourself forward.

I had to ask her to drop the 'Mister' and just call me 'Jack'.

I made it clear that my offer was not an impulsive one.

She smiled so sweetly and a little patronisingly like she might smile at a kid who had offered to marry her.

I felt that I needed to emphasise how serious I was.

'My philosophy is that we only travel this way once and I think we all must make a difference. I have two healthy kidneys. Your lad badly needs one and I am offering. Please don't dismiss the offer'.

Her aspect changed to a more serious one.

I had convinced her of my good faith.

She thanked me most sincerely. The offer was amazingly selfless.

'Have you discussed this with your wife or partner?' She wanted to know.

I told her that I had no wife as yet but I had told my partner and she had voiced no objection to my undergoing the tests anyway. Like all of us, she knew that it was a long shot.

She said that the tests would be quite invasive. There would be blood tests, tissue tests and other such tests.

I told her that I had researched the topic and that I knew what I was letting myself in for.

'We were not thinking of living donors at all. We were pinning our hopes on Alfie gaining a kidney from some poor individual's demise in an accident.'

'So no luck with family, I chanced, sensing that she might now see me as being entitled to enquire.

'No, like Alfie I have just one functioning, kidney. And as Hassan is the stepdad, the tests, not surprisingly, ruled him out.

Then, as if it were an afterthought she added.

'And unfortunately, Alfie's biological father is deceased', she explained, in a matter-of-fact tone.

That was about the measure of it all right.

I was Alfie's best chance, maybe his last and only chance.

'Jack, your offer is generous to a degree that is above and beyond. But if you are serious in your kind offer, I will talk to the medics and tell them about your willingness to do a test'.

That was all I wanted from her.

Chapter 38

Martin contacted Karen again and of course, she agreed to meet him. Jack Reilly knew nothing about this. I think that Karen is about to make a big mistake. She claimed that the only reason she agreed to meet up with him was to dissuade him from contacting her any more. I wanted that to be the case but somehow I doubted it.

She met Martin on a Wednesday night at a hotel in the Dockland area. The meeting was described as being very 'civilised', whatever that means in the context.

'Well, tell me what you discovered'.

'He is definitely single again', she informed me. 'He is separated for three years and has not been seeing anyone since'.

I found this hard to believe but Karen was willing to accept it at face value.

Karen was interested. I could see that.

Time can play tricks on us all.

But had she forgotten all the heartache associated with the same man?

'Any kids?'

'No kids'.

'Did he explain why he two-timed you?' I asked, in an attempt to remind her that he was far from the finished model.

Karen looked a little embarrassed at that subject being raised again but she tolerated my bluntness.

'No, he didn't mention it but I certainly did. I told him that he acted despicably, that he had broken my heart and that I continued to bear the scars of the breakup for years afterwards. I also told him that he destroyed my confidence'.

I was surprised.

'Wow, you fairly landed it on him. Fair play to you! How did he react to all of that?'

Karen seemed surprised by his attitude.

'That's the funny thing. He agreed with me and then he apologised; for all that is worth now. I mentioned that I was in the early days of a new relationship with a kind and decent man, who was doing the right thing by me. I was not going to dump Jack and go running to him, just because he snapped his fingers'.

'Wow, Karen, fair bloody play to you! I didn't think you had it in you. Good on you girl!'

I imagined that Martin had built that into his calculations and had been expecting a bit of a backlash. I believe that being with Jack, gave Karen the courage and the confidence to challenge him. Karen was congratulating herself on sending Martin away with a flea in his ear but I was not so sure. That was only Round One.

I must say that I was proud of Karen. She had done well but I believed that she would have to be on top of her game, if she were to avoid falling victim to that man's charms.

Jack was a great guy, who was kind and understanding with her. He was not a player. He was a nice guy but very often, the villain is the more attractive proposition for a girl and when that villain has looks, charm and lots of money, the playing pitch is never level.

Karen had something else to tell me.

'Jack wants to be tested to see if he could be a living donor, for that boy on dialysis. He told the kid's mother that he would do the tests as soon as they can be arranged. What do you think of that?'

I had to admit that I was shocked. You read of things like that but you seldom see it in your circle of acquaintances.

 'Jesus Karen! That is an incredible thing for a stranger to do. I heard of another man, who did the same a few years ago. As far as I remember, in that case, the patient rejected the kidney after a while.'

Karen hoped that Jack would not be a match.

'It is so kind and selfless', I said, feeling renewed respect for the man.

'Danny was willing to donate every organ after his death but his kidneys had been damaged after the accident'.

Karen wondered what Danny might have thought of her current boyfriend. 'We'd probably be out for meals together. Do you think that they would have got on well?

The same thought had crossed my mind. I knew that Danny had had preconceptions about people but I think that he would have come around to liking Jack.

'Yea, given time, I think that they would have got on well'.

Karen felt much the same. Danny would probably have been a bit over-powering for Jack.

'Yes, we have very different tastes in men'.

Chapter 39

Despite many hours of research, on-line, I was not prepared for the battery of tests. It looked like I was going to become a human pincushion.
There was a full physical examination. The blood test was no big deal. Then there were urine and glucose tolerance tests.
My BMI fell well within the acceptable range. That was one benefit of being a weedy, little nerd. I can tell you that no aspiring astronaut was ever prodded and poked as much. Ultrasound and ECG tests followed but it was the psychological health check that was a big surprise for me. They told me that I would also have to see an independent expert, who would set out all the risks and possible side effects for me.
        Suzi and her husband invited me over to see Alfie. I was delighted to know that he was in excellent spirits but they said that he was physically weak.
Alfie came across as a likeable and serious-minded young fellow. He was a bit like me in that regard and he was an only child.
        I met Suzi's husband, Hassan Ahmadi for the first time. He is a medic and he understood better than I, what was involved in the whole process.
He gave me a warm embrace.
'Thank you for doing so much for our son, for giving him, at least the hope of a normal, healthy life.'
If only he knew the truth.
I was invited to chat to Alfie. He was in his room, watching football videos.
        'Who do you support in soccer?' I asked him. 'No, no, let me guess, you are a Man. United supporter'.

I had presumed that he was like the majority of nine-year-olds in Ireland.

He was indignant.

'No way, I support Liverpool', he proudly declared.

'Oh, Liverpool is it? Don't you think they are a bit overrated? They are not scoring too many goals at the moment.'

He looked at me to see if I was being serious or not.

'They never scored more', he said, for the record.

'What's your team?' he asked me.

'Sligo Rovers' I answered.

He looked at me with derision.

'They are only in the League of Ireland?' he replied.

'Yea, and aren't we in Ireland'?

'We are but Sligo Rovers are not a top football team like Liverpool or Chelsea are,' he explained.

' Don't be insulting me and my team', I laughed.

He laughed as he said it.

If he had insulted my mother, my father and my entire ancestry, I would not have minded. I was so happy that he was even able to talk about football. That interest would keep his mind off his health issues. I made a mental note to buy him some Liverpool merchandise. It would be the first ever present from his dad.

I knew he would have supported Dublin in Gaelic football. There was no difficulty predicting his answer to that.

'Dublin, who else? Come on The Dubs!' he shouted.

Maybe I was being a bit too hasty in agreeing to give away my kidney.

Seriously though, it was just brilliant that he was so into Sport.

'Do you like The Dubs? He asked this, with a look of devilment in his sick-looking eyes.

'I am a proud culchie but I like the way The Dubs are set up. They play attacking and exciting football. I love to watch them in action. They always bring a crowd too. Tell me, do you have the Dublin strip?'

Of course, he had. He also had signed jerseys and his picture with the *Sam Maguire Cup*.

If only I could have identified myself, I would have guaranteed him, not only trip after trip to *Croke Park* but also a trip to a few Liverpool home games at *Anfield*. However, being just a generous teacher, there was no way I could make such an offer. He had a question for me.

'Why do you think that people outside Dublin never support them?'

'It's pure jealousy', I responded. They win so many games, much more than the other teams'.

I asked him a bit about school and I was so thrilled that he enjoyed going there. It was more interesting going to primary school than it was in my day. He told me that he would like to be a teacher when he grew up. I smiled but secretly vowed that I would have a word with him and point him in a different direction.

It was nothing short of marvellous, to have had the opportunity to chat to him on a one-to-one basis. Both Hassan and Suzi kindly invited me to drop in any time. It was an invitation I fully intended to take up.

Chapter 40

I took another step on my road to improved fitness last night
and thoroughly enjoyed it. I finally joined the Athletics Club. It
was great to get out again. I was beginning to feel more human.
We did a few limbering up exercises, before taking to the track
again, even if it was only in short, panting bouts.
Our instructor, Peter Mc Gowan is quite a handsome guy but he
is a bit full of himself. He probably thinks that he is God's gift
to women. He certainly looked good. There was not a spare
ounce on him and he was far from bad looking. I told him that
Jack Reilly had recommended his classes.
'Brilliant! ' He replied. 'Jack is a sound bloke. I don't see a lot
of him at work but we occasionally meet up for a pint.'

I was delighted that I did not know any of the other
participants and that was the way I liked it. The thirteen or
fourteen people, who had enrolled, were all interested in getting
fit and looking better. I enjoyed the workout. I even felt that this
activity could well become the highlight of my week.
That probably said a lot about my social life at the moment.
I left the car park after ten o'clock, with leaden legs and
a rosy complexion. I felt like going straight home for a shower
but I had arranged with Karen that I would visit on my way
home.
I must have looked as if I had finished a half marathon.
'Well, hello, you hot and sweaty thing'.
'One out of two isn't bad and anyway, ladies don't sweat'.
'Maybe you are no lady', she jokingly replied.
'And maybe I would have more fun if I wasn't a lady', I
ventured.

Karen wanted to know how it had gone.

'I really enjoyed it and I did not feel a bit out of place. There were every shape and size there and they all seemed very nice'.

Karen was happy that it had gone well.

'And what did you think of Peter?'

'Well, Karen, I think he fancies himself big-time. I would not trust him'.

'That certainly seems to be his reputation. Jack says that he would get up on a cracked plate'.

I tried not to picture that.

'Anyway, how was your evening?' I asked.

She told me that she had spent the evening curled up in her pyjamas, sitting in front of the television.

'I have a bottle of wine open if you care for a glass'.

I was tempted but felt that I had no option but to decline.

Apart from the fact that I was driving, I did not want to undo my evening's good work.

'Any word from Jack?'

'Yea', she said, checking her mobile. He texted me an hour ago to say that he was leaving that sick lad's house. They put on a nice meal for him'.

'Yea, the Last Supper, so well they might! They have met a rare man in Jack'.

Karen was not looking forward to it.

'Fingers crossed it will not be a match. I don't want him putting himself through that but I sound so selfish,' she added.

She explained that all this was putting pressure on Jack.

'He is on a fitness kick and he's got fierce fussy about what he eats. He imagines that he has to be in peak condition to give away a kidney. If you ask me, they are so stuck for a kidney, they would take one from a steak and kidney pie,' she fumed.

It was clear that she was upset. I suspected that the whole notion of becoming a donor was beginning to drive a wedge between Jack and her.

She practically confirmed as much.

'He's not the same craic anymore Lucy. He was better craic when he was a slob'.

I asked whether she had any word from you-know-who.

That got her interested.

She sat up straight, as she spoke.

'Yes. I was dying to tell you'.

'Tell me, what?'

'Look behind you! See, in the sink there', she said.

I turned around and spied a large bunch of flowers with their roots resting in the water.

I had expected as much.

'Was there a card included?'

There was a card. She handed it to me.

It read:

> *'To: the beautiful Karen, with all my love.*
> *Martin.'*

Pass me the bucket, please!

'Jack won't be too pleased to see those flowers or this soppy card either'.

'He won't see them', she assured me. 'I will bring them into the office tomorrow'.

'I hope you told Martin where to stick his flowers'.

She had not done anything of the sort.

Karen really enjoyed being wooed by this man. It was certainly more exciting than listening to Jack, boring her to death, with all his talk about food supplements.

'Karen, I know that it's great to feel wanted and it's so romantic to be showered with gifts but you have to look at the track record of the man behind those gifts. If he wins you over again, what makes you think that it will end up differently this time?'

'I know, I know', she said rather irritably.

She assured me that she was not weakening in her resolve, with regard to Martin.

'What if Martin's flowers are delivered, when Jack is here? Jack will suspect that you are two-timing him. Nobody likes being made a fool of.'

I gave her a moment to answer that question but she was content to let it pass.

'I believe that Jack is a good bet for the long haul. He loves you and will care for you. It mightn't be in a flashy, exciting way but his love is no less for that. Look here, Karen, he is such a nice bloke that he is offering a kidney to a perfect stranger. Do you think that Martin would give someone a kidney? Not a chance!

Martin would not give you the steam from his cabbage. He will never love anyone more than he loves himself. Until you realise that, I fear you are likely to be fooled by him'.

Karen shifted uncomfortably on the sofa. It was not what she wanted to hear. I am sure there was a part of her that was angry with me but she did not snap back at me.

For my part, I knew that I had rained on her parade. Maybe she needed that but maybe I was going a bit over the top.

Karen, I'm sorry if I am going off on one but I am your friend and certain things need to be said. You have been a terrific friend to me especially since Danny passed. I want to repay some of that to you by being the very best friend I can for you'.

I could see that Karen was becoming slightly emotional. I feared that I had gone a step too far. I was surprised when she got up and approached me. She threw her arms around me. Through her tears, she told me that I was right. She admitted that she was flattered by the attention.

'But you are right, as always. I will text him and ask that he sends no more flowers or anything else for that matter'.

I felt that I had won a battle but Martin was more than capable of winning the war.

Chapter 41

I send Lucy to his fitness class and that reprobate thinks that she is fair game.

I was raging with Peter.

I met him the following day.

'Thanks for sending me that Lucy girl. She is a sexy bit of stuff. What's her story?'

I told him about her losing her husband in a tragic accident, about her descent into the depths of grief and about her baby steps back to normal living. His only response was: 'I'd say she'd be good to go. She must have been missing the regular sex'.

I felt like hitting him but what purpose would that serve? He could never understand why I was being so protective of this random woman.

'Tell me Jack, has she been seeing anyone since her old man cashed in his chips?'

My blood was beginning to boil. He did not give a toss about anyone but himself.

I created the impression that there was a certain colleague, who had been interested in her and insinuated that she had been on a few dates with him. I was being liberal with the truth but I felt that it was in a good cause.

It became clear that Lucy had made a very big impression on him.

'I bet she is gagging for it. Anyway Jack, what sort of bloke was her old man?'

I told him that the word was that Danny Keane was a very sound bloke. He was only in his thirties when he was killed. He had a great career in computer software. If you get a chance to blow your own posthumous trumpet, then I damn well think you should take it.

My eulogy- like praise did not have the intended affect. Like someone else around here, he had his own preconceived notions about those in that particular industry.

'I know what you mean. He was probably one of those computer geeks, who think the world is all about their industry. I'd say that poor woman did not get nearly enough attention when he was around. She will be trying to make up a bit of lost ground', he predicted.

He could never have guessed the impact of his off the cuff remarks on me.

'Did they have kids?' he asked.

'No kids but they were planning to start a family'.

'Yea, see, I was right all along. Wasn't I? These computer guys are up their own arses'.

I had heard enough of this so I moved the spotlight onto him 'Anyone on the scene for yourself, Peter?'

'As the unemployed actors say: 'I'm resting between engagements but there is not a lot of rest, if you follow me. Anyway, I feel that there is something big in the pipeline'.

With that, he continued on his way.

It's hard to think that the anniversary of my death is coming up in a week. At times, it has seemed an awful lot longer and at times, it feels like it was only yesterday that I was involved in that collision. Since then, I have learned more about myself than I had done in the previous thirty-odd years.

It was clear that Lucy had been a martyr to put up with me for as long as she did. I had no idea how controlling and judgmental I had been.

The only way that I can atone for this and make it up to Lucy, is to try to ensure that the rest of her life is happy. That would not be the case if she gets involved with the Romeo of the running tracks. I have to do my utmost to make sure that he doesn't get close to her. She deserves better and I will have to make sure that she gets what she deserves. I will have to do what I can to make it up to her.

I also need to make it up to Alfie. The whole business of the kidney transplant is taking its time. At least I'm doing my best there. I am awful conscious that it might all go belly up but I have my fingers crossed.

I have called to see him a couple of times in recent weeks. I brought him a few football magazines and a Liverpool match programme, which I got a friend to buy for him. He was delighted to get his hands on that. He told me that he can sing all of the Liverpool Anthem: '*You Will Never Walk Alone*'. He is a true Liverpool supporter and a great kid.

I fully intended to buy Liverpool FC gear for him. I might even be buying it in *Anfield*. This is because Karen is talking about taking a city break to the U.K. If we were to go to Liverpool, I could kill two birds with the one stone. Karen could have her exciting weekend and I could get some merchandise for Alfie in the Liverpool Megastore. He would be made up.

That evening I needed to clear my head so I went for a walk in the woods. It was twelve months since Danny Keane passed away. It is very difficult to get your head around the idea that you are a year dead.

My thoughts went back to another significant death in my past, the death of my two parents. It was not as if they were prepared for the crossing from the earthly realm. They went from the sleep of carbon monoxide poisoning to the awakening in a new

195

and strange place. I wondered how long it took them to move on, if they moved on at all. Could they have returned in different guises?

If they had been, I had surely met them. This line of thinking was beginning to drive me mad. I finished my walk and made my way home as the rain began to fall.

Chapter 42

Danny's anniversary mass was going to be a two-day event. I had arranged that there would be an anniversary mass on Friday evening, in Dublin and the second one in Dromahair on Sunday. Those two places had served as the bookends of Danny's life.

Andrew was very kind to me giving me both Friday and Monday off work. Since our 'misunderstanding' he had behaved like a perfect gentleman.

I had intended taking those days as part of my annual leave but Andrew would not hear of it. He even attended the mass in Dublin and was persuaded to come back to the house afterwards. He found it difficult to believe that a year had elapsed since he drove me to the hospital and stayed by my side until Karen arrived.

'I felt so sorry for you. I was shell-shocked and I didn't even know the man. You must have been devastated'.

I had been devastated and a year had not made a huge difference to that.

I was devastated.

'Andrew, thank you again, for all your kindness, then and since. It's only now that I am taking some baby steps in getting my life back.'

Pointing to Jack, he said:

'That gentleman there, told me that you have gone back to the running club. That can only do you good'.

'Oh yea, that's Jack. He's Karen's boy friend. And I hope it will be good but it is tough to pick yourself up again'.

Andrew laid a comforting hand on my shoulder and assured me that he would be there for me. If you ever want a day off, or a chat or maybe some company of an evening, look no further than me'.

He was clearly throwing his hat in the ring if I ever felt like male company again. I was unsure as to whether I could contemplate that.

On Saturday evening, I travelled home to Sligo. Karen and Jack kindly came down as well. They stayed in a hotel on the outskirts of the town. My brother Mark and his girlfriend had booked a restaurant for the family on Saturday night. That was nice. They wanted the occasion to be a celebration of Danny's life.

Mark proposed the toast.

'We will raise a glass to Danny Keane. Gone but not forgotten.'

I told Karen that Andrew had put his name down as a prospective partner.

'Well, that's a big compliment to you. He appears to be a really nice man.'

Karen confided in me that her boyfriend was really impressed by Andrew.

'He was talking to him in your house and after we left, he was bending my ear saying how nice he was.'

It was an interesting observation. I would have thought that Andrew would have kept a lower profile on the night. I was very surprised he came back to the house.

'He must have it bad, this love thing!' Karen joked.

I had never got a chance to get to know Mark's girlfriend until that anniversary weekend. I liked what I saw and I immediately warmed to her. It is said that boys marry girls, who in some way, remind them of their mother. I can't speak for Mark but she certainly reminded me of Mum in so many ways. Hazel had the same dark eyes, the same sweet smile but more than that she appeared to have the same kindness and generosity towards her fellow man.

Hazel had spent a year on voluntary service overseas. She had been based in West Africa and had worked in education there. She described the primitive living conditions and how underfunded the schools were. They barely had materials to write on.

As she spoke, I could see her eyes light up, as she recalled how, even with limited resources, the students had blossomed.

My mum would have loved to work in the Third World. At nineteen years of age, she joined an order of missionary nuns, as a postulant. She stayed for two years before she decided that a celibate life was not for her. She never got to do missionary work abroad.

My dad used to joke about how she always favoured the missionary position.

On Sunday we paraded into the small church at the top of the village in Dromahair. It was not my church but this was where Danny was baptised, where he made his First Communion and also his Confirmation. This place meant something to him. I didn't know any of the worshippers, but of course, in a small place, I was identifiable as Danny Keane's widow. I was a stranger to them but I felt at home because I had married one of their own.

Danny belonged to a family, which had been visited by tragedy in the past. This small church had also held the two coffins of his parents as hundreds of locals paid their final respects to them. My hand was shaken. People spoke to me about how fine a man Danny had been and one or two spoke of his parents. I should have asked the priest to include their names during the service.

I simply had to go out to the townland of Ballyore, to the field where I had scattered Danny's ashes. As was the case on my last visit, I wanted to be alone in that rocky field.

The field looked bare again as it had last year. The recent frost had cut back any attempt of growth. I stood in the field and for a few moments, closed my eyes in silent prayer. Then, as I had done before, I spoke aloud as if my beloved Danny could hear me.

'Danny, I trust that you are at peace. Hopefully, you have been reunited with your mum and dad. I'm still struggling down here but it's getting a little better with every passing day. You can relax about me, Danny. I am getting stronger and will be all right.

'Love you forever, Danny. Sleep tight!

Chapter 43

In Liverpool, I had Karen all to myself. There was none of the weight of expectation or indeed the novelty associated with the Carrick-on-Shannon trip. There is a first time for everything in a relationship and when some scary firsts are out of the way, the pressure is lifted.

Karen and I had been getting on really well. We had a good relationship as friends but also as lovers. Despite all of that, I have to admit that I have been a bit preoccupied of late. The whole business about Alfie's illness had got to me and Lucy's predicament was also giving me cause for concern.

Karen has not been her usual self either. I'm not sure what the issue is but I think that she has an issue with my concerns for Lucy's welfare. I have deliberately sought to paint Peter in a poor light, because I feel that a relationship with him, would be disastrous for Lucy. In my opinion, he is a sexual predator. I have not been shy in spelling out his shortcomings when chatting to Karen. My hope is that she might advise Lucy away from him. Karen has a principled objection to this however as she feels that Lucy must form her own opinions on the man. I will have to try to be subtler in future.

On the night of my own anniversary mass, I made it my business to chat with Andrew. In the past, I could never imagine myself going anywhere near the man but circumstances dictated otherwise. Andrew might not be the man I would pick out for Lucy but I feel that he is a more decent sort than Peter can ever be. Andrew has shown himself to be caring and understanding of her. Peter does not even know the meaning of the words. I put out the word that Andrew had created a great impression on me and that he was one hell of a guy. I don't know if I was fooling anybody but you can't blame a man for trying.

Coming to Liverpool provided an opportunity to get to *Liverpool FC Megastore* and buy some club merchandise for Alfie. I felt sure that he would really treasure anything from the club store. I didn't want Karen to get the idea that it was all about him, so I kept quiet on it until we were nearly heading home. As far as she was concerned, this trip was a bonding exercise for the two of us, away from our normal distractions.

We stayed in really convenient accommodation near *The Echo Arena*, overlooking Albert Dock. That was the red-bricked, rejuvenated, waterside area of the city. It had become a tourist hub in recent years. This is the beating heart of their tourist area. It was filled with bars and restaurants with hen and stag parties tripping over each other. There was also a surprising richness as regards cultural sites, with many museums and art galleries. Karen was fascinated with the slavery exhibition and for me; the Titanic Museum held great appeal.

The *One* Shopping area was on our doorstep. This was brilliant, considering that Karen loved a bit of retail therapy. A lovely Italian restaurant caught our eye but on checking it out, we learned that it would be an hour before we could expect our table. We put our name down for a table and enjoyed a drink in one of the local hostelries until the table was ready.

True to their word, our table was ready and as soon as we entered we were shown to the table. Our waitress was a Galway girl, who was studying Science in Liverpool and was earning a few pounds at the weekends. This girl immediately detected that we were from Ireland.

'Are ye over for the shopping or a match?

I explained that we had heard so much about the city and wanted to sample it for ourselves.

'That won't take very long but the shopping is really good. Football is a big thing in the city from August to May. Are ye into football at all?'

Karen wasn't but I told her that I followed the fortunes of Liverpool FC.

'Can I walk to *Anfield* from here?' I asked.

She would not advise that.

'I wouldn't! It's about three and a half miles out. I walked once with my boyfriend but I had heels on and it nearly killed me. Get the bus or take a taxi.'

I asked her whether her boyfriend was Irish.

'No, he's French.'

Karen seemed impressed by that.

'Wow, that is so cool. I think French men are so sexy and good-looking' she enthused.

The waitress had an open mind on that one.

'Maybe they are good looking but the problem is they know it. Thankfully my fellow is more like an Irish lad. He has no interest in clothes, no clue of style and he is good craic'.

'Are you sure he's French?' I asked.

'Well, his mother is from the States so I suppose he is not one hundred per cent French.'

Karen was always interested in hearing about how couples met up.

'Do you know how the American lady met his dad?'

The Galway girl checked her watch.

'I am going to be on a fifteen minute break soon, so if it's ok with you folks, I will pull in a chair and join you'.

Karen and I looked at each other.

Politeness only allowed for one answer to that question, so within ten minutes, our table for two had become a table for three.

Meghan was the girl's name and she was keen to chat.

'This place is very busy. It obviously has a good reputation, Karen remarked.

Meghan was not too sure.

'Yea, it gets good reviews but I think it's overrated. There are loads of better places, all around the place'.

Her frankness was refreshing, if not disconcerting.

'We waited an hour for this table', I told her.

She looked at us, rather sympathetically.

'You better make the most of it so'.

Meghan was a vivacious and likeable chatterbox but she was not a great ambassador for the establishment.

Karen brought the conversation back to how her prospective parents-in-law had met.

We learned that they had met at a party in Manhattan and they immediately clicked. They had a bit of a fling but she found out that he had done the dirt on her. She left him. He continued to sow his wild oats for another few years. The two were destined to bump into each other at JFK airport. Despite the initial frostiness, they had an enjoyable couple of hours together. They kept in contact. He employed his full repertoire of charms on her and over time she relented.

'It was meant to be', Karen declared.

It was a sort of real-life *Mills and Boon* story for her.

I just wished that Meghan had left us to our own devices.

After fifteen minutes her break was up and I got my wish.

Karen harked back to that story on a few occasions that evening. She was an incurable romantic.

'Jack, do you believe in fate? I mean, do you believe that in life, there is one person, who you are destined to be with'?

It was an interesting question but I don't think that I would subscribe to that notion.

'I know that a lot of people have this idea that 'what is for you won't go past you' but I think that we make our own decisions for good or ill.

'So you can't say in looking back over your life that there has been a sort of divine plan that was playing out your destiny?'

'Maybe, you have a point there'.

I was certainly the wrong man to go arguing against her on that point.

We had a lovely evening together, which we rounded off with a quiet drink and an early night in our very cosy bed. On this occasion, I had ordered champagne for the room and both of us were in great spirits. Things were going well between us and I was pleased about that. It is not every day that a man can report that he scored in an away encounter at Liverpool.

We chilled a bit and strolled around the city in the morning and enjoyed lunch in the shopping centre. I had expected that Karen would remain shopping in the city while I took a taxi out to the stadium but she was game to go out to the stadium.

Once in *Anfield*, I nipped into the megastore. I rooted around to see what might be most appropriate for him. Eventually, I bought an *Away* shirt, a tracksuit and a cute little hoodie in club colours.

I passed on the stadium tour, as that would have been very unfair on Karen.

As I was taking a final look around the place, Karen received a text from Lucy. She read it and let out a cry of surprise. I wondered what this might be. She handed me the mobile to read the text for myself.

*Randy Andy came round last night with a bottle of Sancerre and chocolates. I was dumbfounded. Awkward at first but we got on well.*
*Am I a fool or what? LOL*

 So, Andrew was about to stake his claim. It was interesting that he had allowed the anniversary to pass before he made his move. He didn't hang around after that. Andrew probably subscribed to the philosophy that a faint heart never won the fair lady and had opted to take a calculated risk. Part of me was jealous of him and another part of me was pleased. It would have been so much worse, had her message began: *Peter came round*
That would have been an unmitigated disaster.

Chapter 44

Karen seemed to have enjoyed Liverpool. She was surprised at my text. She mentioned that she showed it to Jack. That was interesting, considering that she didn't show him Martin's *'Thinking of you'* message.

I had given up warning her against him, as I didn't want to sound like a stuck record. Anyway, I felt it could well be counter-productive. She knew exactly where I stood on the matter and after all, she was a big girl, who should know her mind. She told me about the Irish waitress in Liverpool and she especially latched on to the story of the couple reuniting after several years of being apart. She was being highly selective in what she focused on.

As for my troubled relationships, I was really surprised that Andrew risked making a cold call on me. I had been half expecting a repeat invite to drinks from him but he summoned up sufficient courage to ring my doorbell, unannounced. He looked more than a little coy and shifty, half-expecting to be on the receiving end of another thumping from me.

He even used the same opening sentence.

'I come in peace!'

'At least, he did not insult my intelligence by claiming that he was just passing or was in the area.

'I thought you could do with some company and I know that I certainly could'.

There is no question but that we are alike: two lonely and vulnerable people, alone on a Friday night. This was not a scenario that I would have orchestrated but after my battering him, I felt safe. I doubted that he would try anything on.

He is a decent sort but I could never see him as a sexual partner or indeed a life partner. My fear always was that we are looking for very different things from the relationship. Maybe I was over-thinking the whole business.

Anyway, I am beginning to put some shape on my life. I am looking after my appearance and my diet. I am glad to report that I have lost some weight. As regards general fitness, I have a fair bit to go yet. I went to the fitness classes again this week and found it really useful. We are all on first name terms and there is a very easy relationship among the lot of us.

Peter, the instructor is a bit of a showman. He struts around the gymnasium, displaying his well- toned body like a teenage boy at the Rugby Club disco. I would guess that he uses his classes as a place to pick up eligible females. I may be useless at reading signals but I felt that he was about to make a move on me. I'm not an impressionable young girl but I take that as a really encouraging sign as well as a great boost to my ego. It appears that I'm still an attractive female and can pull the men yet. Two men showing interest in me within a few days of each other: That can't be all bad.

Through the evening Peter had been giving me the glad-eye but it was only when I was getting ready to leave that he mentioned, what had clearly been exercising his thoughts.

' Is Jack Reilly your minder or what?' he asked.

'What are you on about?' I asked.

His face bore a quizzical look.

'Well, last week when I mentioned that you were doing well in the class, Jack turned very nasty and warned me to stay away from you'.

'I haven't a clue what you are on about,' I replied.

'Oh, it was as if he was your security detail'.

I was really annoyed with Jack for interfering like this in my private life.

'That is absolute nonsense', I replied. 'He hardly knows me. He has no interest in me and I certainly have no interest in him'.

'I will take your word on that but who is this Andrew bloke? Jack gave me the impression that you and this bloke have something going on.'

This was getting even more ridiculous. I wondered what on earth Jack was up to.

'What Andrew bloke?' I asked, reddening with embarrassment.

Jack Reilly seemed to take great liberties. He was overstepping the mark.

The more I thought about it, the angrier I became.

Whereas I was reddening before, I was now boiling mad.

I hated this sort of interference, no matter how well intentioned it may be.

I put Peter straight on both Jack and Andrew.

'Not that it is any of your business but I have nothing to do with this Andrew man. He is my boss and that is all there is to it'.

Peter, for his part, seemed pleased that I was a free agent. He gave his trademark, cheeky-chappie smile and asked:

'So, you might be free to come out for a drink with me tomorrow night'.

I would have done anything at this stage to spite Jack

'I might well be', I answered.

Peter gave me the thumbs up sign and said that he would meet me in Murphy's at eight.

'Meet me outside in the car park', I requested.

I did not want to be hanging around the bar on my own, like a loner waiting for a man, who might or might not show up.

I always hated that sort of loose arrangement.

'The car park it is', he acknowledged.

That was tomorrow night's agenda but before that, there was one item to be dealt with tonight yet.

I called into Karen's place on the way home on the off chance that the interfering and meddlesome Jack might be there. As luck would have it, he was there with her, sitting on the sofa watching television with a look of innocence about him. You would think that butter would not melt in his mouth!

I skipped the formalities and immediately went on the attack.

'I have a bone to pick with you, Jack Reilly'.

His look was one of pure shame, like a kid who had been caught rummaging in his granny's handbag.

He knew that the game was up.

I did not spare him. I was only sorry that Karen had to witness it.

She seemed disappointed that it had come to this with Jack. He did not attempt to deny anything, merely to excuse it.

'Peter Mc Gowan preys on women. I could not let him prey on you, especially when you are so vulnerable'.

That was it for me. I let fly.

'So you think that I am vulnerable. Who on earth do you think you are, Jack Reilly, to presume anything about me? Who are you anyway? You don't know me at all. How dare you presume to manage my social life.'

'But I felt that I had a certain responsibility to look out for you', he protested.

'You have no responsibility where I am concerned. I just want you to butt the hell out of my life, unless you want a kick you know where'.

He visibly flinched but I was not finished.

'If you ever stick your nose into my business again, I will come for you. And it won't be pretty. You have enough to do to keep Karen happy.'

I could see Karen wince as I made that point. That was unfair of me.

I was sorry that I had mentioned her at all.

Jack looked like a little, whipped puppy.

I was mad with him but I felt that I might have gone overboard.

Karen then came to Jack's defence.

'Listen, Lucy, I know you are mad with Jack and I understand that. I agree that he was out of order but I know he genuinely thought that he was acting in your interests,' she explained.

I knew that she was right but I was too angry to acknowledge that Jack offered his apology and again tried to rationalise his decision.

'You should hear the crude things Peter Mc Gowan says about women and all he is going to do with them'.

I had heard enough from Jack.

'Drop it Jack, I am a big girl and you need not have any worries about me on that score. And another thing, what on earth, were you telling him about me and Andrew?'

This served only to increase his embarrassment.

Even Karen seemed to have been taken by surprise by this. She gave him a sharp, disapproving dig in the ribs.

Jack had no choice but to come clean.

'OK, I will hold my hands up to that. I mentioned Andrew just to put Peter off the scent'.

This was going from bad to worse.

'You take an awful bloody lot on yourself,' I remarked in exasperation.

Jack had presumed a great deal and although I had cooled down, I still wanted to let him know that I was not going to be deflected from doing whatever I wanted to do. His opinion on the matter was of no consequence to me.

'And for your information, I have agreed to go on a date with Peter Mc Gowan tomorrow evening, so you can put that in your pipe and smoke it.'

I left on that note, feeling pretty sure that Karen was about to tear into him as well.

I think Jack has learned his lesson.

It had been an eventful evening.

Chapter 45

Lucy gave me an awful roasting. When she left, Karen gave me an even bigger roasting.

The fact that I have to hide my real interest in Lucy means that I am on a hiding to nothing. Sad to say but my relationship with both women is a bit of a disaster area at the moment.

My fears about Peter are well founded. I hope Lucy doesn't see Peter as having anything to offer her. Any relationship with him would surely end in tears and they would not be his tears. I hope Lucy doesn't become a victim of her own loneliness and possibly, view Peter as having something to offer her. I am frustrated that I cannot do more for her.

On another front, definite progress can be reported. It has been confirmed that I am a very good match as a kidney donor for Alfie, but I can't take any credit for that. I have not told Karen yet. She probably won't be pleased but what a man has to do, a man has to do.

I will have to mention it soon because I have to go into hospital for more tests, in advance of the surgery. I know that she has her reservations on the matter. I would love to have her blessing but it is something that I am going to do anyway.

Hopefully, all this will be the beginning of a new lease of life for Alfie and spell an end to his misery of dialysis. It will be a massive weight off my mind if it works for him but there are no guarantees. At least, I will have done all that I possibly could to help the little chap.

Hassan and Suzi will compensate me any way they can. Nothing would be too much bother for them. They would erect a statue to me in their front garden if someone suggested it.

Alfie is beginning to hope again. His dad is giving him something to look forward to. He has arranged that he, Alfie and I will travel to Liverpool for a home game as soon as we are fit to travel. It will be a no-expense spared trip, with first class accommodations and premium match tickets. Hassan had suggested a corporate package but Alfie wanted to be among the real fans in the stand, so he won out. I think that Hassan is fine with that now. That is a day I am really, really looking forward to. Who knows, maybe Hassan might be called away to some urgent case on that day? If Alfie and I were to travel there together, then as the expression goes, I can die happy.

I was surprised to learn that Alfie and I will undergo surgery in two different Dublin hospitals. Presuming the repeat blood tests are fine, then the operation will take place by keyhole surgery. They are calling it 'laparoscopic surgery'. You learn something new every day.

I have also been advised to inform my employer that I will be out of work for up to twelve weeks. I have been told that recovery time is not as long or as painful as it used to be with the traditional surgical method, so at least, that is one other upside.

Most of my colleagues are being very supportive. Peter would be in a minority of one. He was setting out to rile me and provoke me. Luckily the encounter took place in the school car park after the kids had departed. I had been deliberately avoiding him but he saw me and, of course, the taunting began.

'Lucy has me killed out. The long lay-off has just whetted her appetite.'

I should not have risen to his bait but unfortunately, I did.

'You are deluded. She wouldn't piss on you, if you were on fire', I said with as much contempt as I could muster.

He had a smug expression on his face. He instinctively knew what buttons to press.

'Actually, it was Lucy who was on fire. Man! Was she hot!' he teased.

I felt like lashing out at him but thankfully, I had some self-control left. He would have liked to provoke me into making a complete fool of myself.

'Anyway Jack, thanks for putting her my way. And you know, that I am only doing her a favour because the poor woman was deprived and she was gagging for it. Not surprising, considering the nerd that she was married to!'

He could never have guessed the impact of that throwaway remark.

'Mocking the dead! That is a new low, even for you. Do you know something? You're a pathetic excuse for a man. Any woman who gets involved with you, would need to have her head examined'. I charged.

He passed that criticism off with a sneering look.

'Funny, Jack, it wasn't her head that needed seeing to.'

I had heard enough from him.

Peter kept up the tirade of abuse as I made my way across the car park.

'Run away, boy and leave the servicing of real women to real men'.

Two hours later and Karen could still see my agitation. I filled her in on the car park incident. She was in no mood to give me any sympathy.

215

'If you were a fish, you would not survive five minutes in the water because you would rise to any bait. Can't you see that the man was just trying to wind you up and you fell for it?'

She was right. That is exactly what had happened.

Maybe it was just empty bluster that he was engaged in.

'You don't think that Lucy let him anywhere near her. Do you?'

Boy, was that a mistake?

She snapped at me viciously.

'Here we go again. Why on earth does Lucy Keane matter to you? Answer me that! A body would think that you fancied her yourself.'

With every word spoken, her voice was growing louder and shriller.

Why could I not keep my mouth shut?

'Is she the real object of your desire?'

Karen felt slighted and I could understand her feelings.

She deserved better from me. I had been so insensitive.

I would have been incandescent with rage if Lucy showed undue interest in another man.

I decided that this might be a good time to apologise and then change the topic of conversation.

'Karen, I am very sorry if you think that way but you are wrong. I sincerely apologise. I have been totally distracted today because I got the message that it's all go for the operation. It seems that I am a good match for this Alfie lad'.

Her mouth hung open in shock.

'Are you seriously telling me that you intend risking your life or future health for a kid, that you barely know?'

I tried my best to explain to her but even to my ears. It all sounded rather hallow.

'Cop yourself on. No one will blame you or think any less of you. You can blame me. Say that I was against it. I don't mind being the big bad witch'.

I could sympathise with her position and would have done the same, were our situations to be reversed.

Regardless of what might be said or done, the dye was cast. I was going under the knife for Alfie.

Chapter 46

Karen is worried about Jack undergoing surgery.

The risks have been explained and they scare her. I suspect that the whole business has driven a wedge between them. I hope they can survive it. There are no guarantees that the operation will even work for the young lad.

She believes that this entire kidney business has shown her a less appealing side to Jack.

'What annoys me most Lucy, is how stubborn he can be. I never saw that in him before and it scares me. He is not the man I fell in love with'.

Jack was deaf to all her concerns. He was like a man on a mission.

Looking back, both of us agreed that he had been behaving quite strangely in the weeks since the anniversary mass in February.

'And who is this kid to him anyway? I asked, giving voice to my own view.

'A very good question! He is not even a student of his. He is just a random pupil.'

'What's his name? I asked.

'It's Alfie something or other. It's a foreign surname, Iranian, I think'.

Karen gave voice to a suspicion that Jack could be the father of the child. Why else would he be so passionate about a stranger?

That seemed incredible but it would make all the pieces of the jigsaw fit. However, she was forgetting one important point.

'He wasn't a perfect match but a very good one. I am no medic but is it not the case that a father would be likely to be more than a good match?'

She had not considered that but she still felt that there was something odd about the whole affair.

I thought that it was only proper that I apologise again for my onslaught on Jack, after my training session.

She seemed to think that he deserved some criticism.

I got the distinct impression that the relationship between her and Jack may have run its course. Karen seemed rather deflated about nearly everything concerning Jack.

'Is there trouble in Paradise? I asked.

'It was never Paradise and it is certainly not Paradise now', she retorted.

'And while we are on about my man, what's the story with you and the infamous Peter? Few would put ye two together', she declared.

I could not argue with that.

'You are probably right. We could never really be an item. We are just having a bit of a laugh. Nothing serious and I can promise you there won't be anything serious either. Peter is great gas but he is not a keeper and he most certainly is not husband material.'

'You are probably right Lucy but can't you use him to practise on until someone better comes along?'

I had to laugh at this especially coming from her.

'I am getting no practice and neither is Peter, no matter what Jack thinks or Peter insinuates. You know me better than that.

'I do indeed. But are you not put out, when you hear back that he is boasting about bedding you and all that?'

'I don't like it and to be honest, I only went out with him at the start because I was so angry with Jack'.

Karen was amused to hear that.

'It's funny the effect he has on women'.

I mentioned to her that Mark and his girlfriend had met Peter, when they were in town.  They had not said so, in as many words but I was left in no doubt but that they disapproved.

'Mark could barely bring himself to make small talk with him and Hazel had a face on her as she had stepped in dog poo. Peter is hardly the babe magnet that he thinks he is'.

'You really admire Hazel, don't you Lucy?'
'I do admire her. She is so nice, so kind and so bloody selfless. Those are rare qualities to find in anyone today'.
'Very rare,' Karen agreed.
'We have all become very selfish'.
Those last six words were throwaway in nature but they contained distilled wisdom. Without intending to, she had hit the nail on the head. For her, it might have just been a throwaway remark. The words echoed and re-echoed in my mind.

Karen told me that Martin had sent a bunch of red roses to her office on three occasions in the last ten days. The fact that he sent them wasn't at all surprising for me. What was surprising was that she managed to keep it to herself for so long.
'You kept that quiet' I remarked.
She had her reasons for doing so.
'When one's boyfriend is doing something selfless and heroic, it's not the time for his girlfriend to be fraternising with her ex'.
That was a good point.
Martin was playing a clever game.
He was wearing her down her resistance.
I could see that he was about to make his move and claim his woman.

'Martin doesn't give up easily. He is trying to wear you down bit by bit'.

She nodded agreement.

'And do you know my problem right now? She asked.

'No, tell me! '

'He is bloody well succeeding', she sighed.

Chapter 47

D-Day, for me, was March 21. Appropriately, it happened to be the Spring Equinox with its promise of better days ahead. This would hopefully be deliverance for young Alfie from the restrictions of dialysis. For me, it would be deliverance from the enormous guilt and helplessness, which I had felt since the accident. I could never be a father to him but I could give him the gift of life. If things went well, I could still play a very central role in his life and there would be a life-long bond between us.

I was heading into unchartered territory. I was tested like an astronaut, who was about to be blasted into space. It was a really exciting adventure. There were risks and no guarantees.

I missed Lucy at times like this. In my previous existence, she would be by my side, holding my hand and assuring me that all would be well. Even, if I had lived and confessed the existence of a son, would she have stood by my side or would she have left me?

Deep down, I felt that while she might well be angry in the short term, she would have come round in the end but that mattered little now.

Karen has been in to visit. She has been the one holding my hand although she does not support my decision. She is definitely a woman of integrity. I know she will support me through the operation and its aftermath. I respect her for that. I hope that when the dust settles on this transplant business, we still can have a relationship together. She has grown in my estimation and I sincerely hope that I am not declining in her estimation.

The operation, I have been informed, will take two to three hours to complete. When one is knocked out, time does not matter. I have been warned that when I eventually awaken, I will feel sore and groggy. I will also have numerous tubes attached to me. I would be surprised at any other scenario. The kidney, once removed, will be taken at high speed, to the hospital where Alfie will be waiting. Time will be of the essence. I can only hope and pray that there will be no complications.

As always, the waiting is the worst. I was anxious to be put under and get things started but there were so many preliminaries. Apart from medical tests, I had to sign several forms, which were a myriad of disclaimers and acceptance of what had been explained to me. I had to put down the name of my next of kin. I named Karen. It was so strange not to be putting down my wife's name but such is life or more correctly, such is death.

The hospital chaplain visited just before I was to be prepped. He sat with me and spoke to me. He asked me whether I was religious or not.

'Yes Father, I am a believer in this world and in the next world too'

'You will find few agnostics working down in the mines or undergoing major surgery in operating theatres. Well, not until they are safely out of the woods anyway', he joked.

He praised me for what I was doing and he called it inspirational.

I felt such a fraud.

He enquired as to whether I wanted to make my confession before I went to the theatre. I told him that I would like to do so. With that, he took his purple stole from his jacket pocket, kissed it and placed it around his neck.

I recited the Confiteor along with him. I needed his help with that one. While I knew the air of it, the words threw me a little. I was a bit rusty where prayers were concerned, especially the longer ones.

When it came to confessing my sins, I made a clean breast of things. I confessed to God that I had been selfish and self-centred. I did not show sufficient love nor did I always treat people with the respect they deserved. The priest did not probe any of these responses. He merely asked: Are you sorry for these sins?'

I answered in the affirmative and I was given absolution.

I had the consolation of feeling that my slate had been wiped clean. The priest told me that he would pray for a successful outcome of the operation. He then blessed me and shook my hand.

'Good luck and may God bless you'.

'And you too Father', I responded automatically.

The porters were in waiting to wheel me to the theatre.

'Showtime', I whispered to myself. 'Bring it on!'

Chapter 48

Karen texted me to say that Jack was out of the theatre and was back on the ward. She was one relieved lady. I was relieved that she was relieved. She had never left the hospital but divided her time between the little oratory on the first floor and the canteen on the ground floor. I volunteered to sit with her but she declined my offer. She wanted to be alone.

The wait must have seemed a veritable eternity to her.

She had texted me regularly throughout the wait. I hoped that I had been some support for her. I suspected that Karen was performing one of her final acts of friendship for Jack. They had endured a very stressful time recently. The nature of their relationship had changed and not for the better. The fact that Karen had a second and ostensibly more attractive admirer, lurking in the background, might also have been a factor.

Karen, however, had a great sense of duty. If Jack had come out of the surgery with any injury or disability Karen would be by his side. If Jack could resume independent living rather quickly, I would not bet on her staying with him.

From my viewpoint, Martin did not seem a good long- term bet but maybe the leopard can change his spots. I have said my piece and will say no more on the matter. I am after all, her friend not her mother. As an intelligent and mature woman, she should know her mind.

I learned that when Jack regained consciousness, he was a bit groggy and very sore. When he opened his eyes, it was appropriate that the first person he saw was the woman, who had kept the long vigil with him.

He was pleased.

' Karen, you are a sight for sore eyes. Thank you for waiting. You are so good'.

Karen confessed that her heart melted with those words. She is an uncomplicated woman. All a man has to do, to impress her, is to throw a few kind words or pay her a nice compliment. I presumed that she smiled her sweet smile and gently touched his hand. When he became more lucid, he enquired about Alfie and was buoyed up by the news of the boy's successful operation. Likewise, the little lad's parents had already been on the phone, anxious to hear how Jack was faring.

'I would love to see him. If I could just get out of this bed!' he declared.

'No way', Karen insisted.' You're not getting out of that bed, no matter how you feel. You have just had major surgery, in case you forgot'.

'I suppose you are right, Karen but it's a bummer being stuck here so far away from him'.

'You have done your good deed for him. That is all that you can do. You have to focus on yourself now', she advised.

He felt so grateful for Karen's support.

'Karen, you and I have to go away somewhere nice after this, for a good long holiday. Maybe we could travel around Ireland. I think we deserve restful time together'.

'Let's focus on your recovery and leave talk of plans until then', Karen suggested.

She felt sorry for him and thought that, by way of compensation, she should offer to visit the young lad.

Jack was thrilled and appreciative.

'That would be brilliant. Thank you so much and make sure to tell him that I was asking for him and tell him that I'm in great form'.

226

This was when I came into the picture. My instinct had always been to refuse anything, which takes me out of my comfort zone. However, Karen's earlier remark on selfishness had struck a chord with me. I agreed to her request to accompany her on that trip to visit the recovering kid.

We could not go for some days but waited until Alfie was adjudged to be over the worst of the initial trauma of the operation. I could not but be moved, when I gazed at his small shape in the big, hospital bed. He looked so small and so vulnerable lying there. A good-looking little fellow, he reminded me a little of what Danny might have looked like at that age. Thanks to Jack, he had now every chance of growing up and living a normal life. Jack had done a great thing.

Alfie's parents never left the place. They were still on *Cloud Nine* and could not speak highly enough of Jack's sacrifice. They asked Karen to relay their eternal gratitude to Jack.

Among all these brave people, I felt a fraud.

Alfie's mother was crying tears of relief and joy. She could hardly believe her luck. She must have feared that it was all just a happy dream, from which she might be rudely awakened. Her husband, Hassan was also buzzing with excitement and gratitude.

Nevertheless, he was being quite circumspect. The first major hurdle had been surmounted but the danger of rejection would, of course, be a risk for some considerable time. He was relieved to learn that Jack was faring well.

'We owe so much to that man'.

Hassan then got into deep in conversation with his wife. On my other side, Karen was chatting away with Alfie. She was telling him about how Jack was looking forward to their Liverpool trip together.

I felt that it was no place for me. I sneaked out for a little stroll on the corridor. It had huge glass windows, which framed Dublin's wonderful skyline. I stood there, struggling to identify the various landmarks. I could see *Liberty Hall* and *The Spire* quite easily as well as the cranes down in the *Docklands*.

I became aware of footsteps coming from the direction of the ward. I turned around, thinking that it might be Karen, coming to meet me.

I turned to face her.

It was not Karen. It was Alfie's dad.

When he was level with me, he pointed to the view and smiled.

'Magnificent, isn't it?

'My son is a lucky boy. He can now look forward to working and living his life, out there in this magnificent city. He will no longer be tethered to a dialysis machine'.

'That's true, I replied. 'He was lucky to have met such a hero as Jack'.

'And the amazing thing is that we were total strangers to him', he replied.

It was certainly an incredible act of selflessness.

Hassan was a relieved man. This was reflected in his expansive mood.

To my surprise, he painted the background for me even though I was a total stranger.

'It looked hopeless for such a long time. Suzi has just one kidney so that was her out. I am not the biological father and I was not a match. It was all looking terribly bleak. Alfie was fading, with each passing week. We were growing more frustrated by the day. The poor boy had to give up on everything a young boy enjoys doing. We prayed so hard for a donor.'

It was a dam burst of emotion. His expressive eyes reflected the relief and joy, which were in his heart. He was not the boy's father but his depth of love for his child was not in doubt.

'It must have been a total nightmare for you all', I suggested.

' Yes it was. Then, there was the tragedy with the biological father'.

He could tell from my puzzled expression, that I was not au-fait with that part of the story.

'Well, back in February, my wife, Suzi, made contact with Alfie's real father. The poor man did not even know that he had a child. My wife and he had split up before she discovered that she was pregnant. My wife could see no compelling reason to have him involved. Anyway, this man got the shock of his life, when Suzi eventually broke the news to him'.

I was intrigued.

This story was taking on new momentum.

'Suzi said that he turned white in the face but in fairness to him, he immediately volunteered his kidney. His worry was how his wife might take it.

Hassan was still in full flow, detailing every stage in the process.

'And then, just when our hopes had been raised, they were dashed, when at the end of that very day, the poor man was dead. It looked like the gods were conspiring against us'.

Wow! Talk about bad luck! My heart went out to this couple, having their hopes dashed so very cruelly.

'What happened the poor man? ' I asked.

I figured that maybe the shock had precipitated a heart attack or a stroke.

I was wrong.

Hassan explained it to me.

'No, he died in a road accident but to add insult to the injury, his kidneys could not be used. The doctor's said that they had been compromised in the accident'.

The tragic story was beginning to draw me into its plot.

'This accident, where did it happen? I asked.

He pointed his arm to the window behind me.

'It was just off the motorway. And would you believe that the poor man was taken from his grieving wife on Valentine's Day of all days,' he sighed.

Oh God! This was taking a twist, I had never anticipated.

My blood ran cold in my veins. I felt my legs grow weak and I was becoming increasingly light-headed. My legs gave way.

I reached for the wall, for support.

I do not remember what happened next.

I must have passed out as the next thing I remember was sitting in a chair with a small crowd around me.

Chapter 49

 People think that I'm a hero but I am nothing of the sort. However, that is something I have to live with.

Karen was at my bedside when I woke up after surgery. She seemed pleased to see me. The poor girl must have been worried about me. I wished that I could have spared her that. There was so little I could tell her.

She had been a bit distracted recently but I'm sure she was apprehensive about the upcoming surgery.

I wanted to see Alfie but that was out of the question.

Karen volunteered to visit him when his doctors allowed her to do so. She would pass on my good wishes. Some hours after she had left my ward, I found myself being overwhelmed by a wave of tiredness. My eyelids became leaden. I could not keep them open. It was then that the now-familiar churning sensation hit me and I knew that higher forces were again at work. I was on the move again but I had no idea where I was going. I hoped that my time back on earth was not coming to an end. I wasn't ready to go yet.

However, I was worrying unduly. As the turbulence ceased, I found myself on a hospital corridor. I was as expected, in invisible mode.

I was shocked and saddened to see a deathly pale Lucy, slumped on a chair. She was being attended to by a couple of nurses. Karen was looking on. She had a very concerned look. What had happened here?

Lucy gradually regained consciousness. One of the nurses gave her an encouraging pat on the shoulder before returning to her duties. The drama seemed to be over. Lucy had passed out for some reason but it had been no medical emergency.

I observed Lucy making her way along the corridor towards the exit. Karen was keeping a cautious eye on her.

It seemed that I was going to see my little Alfie, after all. I was directed down a corridor to the ward, where his bed was. Going through the door, I was delighted to see that he was awake and sprightly looking. His dad was with him. I felt a surge of gratitude that I had been permitted to assist him in his hour of need. I felt joy in my heart. It was as if I had never done anything worthwhile in my entire life up until now.

I didn't get to linger long in the hospital ward. There was something more for me to see or witness. On this occasion, I found myself, being pulled in a downward motion. When I got my bearings again, I was surprised to discover that I was in the back seat of Lucy's car. She was in the front seat alongside Karen. Neither lady was aware of my presence.

Their conversation was quite animated. Lucy was doing the talking and Karen was listening. As I tuned into that conversation, it became clear that Lucy had come into sensational new information and was sharing it with Karen. Anxiety was etched all over her face and her tone was a most serious one.

She told Karen that Alfie's biological father had been killed in a car crash on St. Valentine's Day. Incredibly, it was the same day, on which he learned that he was the kid's father.

The two women looked at each other in horror.

Apparently, the penny had dropped for them.

If I were visible, my expression would have been one of horror also. The pieces of the jigsaw were being put together and the emerging picture was a very disconcerting one for Lucy.

She was growing increasingly angry and feisty. She was threatening to go back to the hospital and have it out with Suzi.

Karen cautioned against such a move, especially considering the fragile state that Suzi was in.

Lucy was now in full flow.

'I bet Danny had been going out with her. I'm pretty sure of it. If that were the case, he had no idea that he had fathered a child. It was most likely that he heard the news of the child on Valentine's Day', she figured

Her powers of deduction were gaining momentum. She was off again.

She had been assiduously assembling the pieces in her mind.

Lucy was growing increasingly animated. Her voice was raised and her face bore a pained expression.

'Karen, it all makes sense now like it never did before. It must have been for a meeting with her, that Danny left the office. He had the accident on the way back. If he had heard, what we think he heard at that meeting, then his head would have been all over the place. It would explain how a careful driver, as he was, would suddenly miss the traffic lights changing to red'.

Lucy had successfully joined the dots and it was causing her great torment. I felt sorry for her.

I also felt guilty and sad that I inadvertently caused her such distress.

Suzi was getting most of her blame.

'Karen, that woman was the cause of Danny's death. He would be alive today if it had not been for her actions. Oh God, oh God, I could kill her'.

Karen cautioned her against jumping to premature conclusions.

'Now now!' Karen said soothingly.

'Maybe we are just letting our imaginations run away with us. Maybe some other bloke was killed that day and maybe he was Alfie's father'.

Lucy was too smart to fall for that.

Her eyes opened wider. Her mouth was open and her two index fingers were raised to signal a 'Eureka' moment.

'Oh Karen! 'I have it now. It was definitely Danny. I have it now. I have it all. It is true. We are not imagining anything'.

Karen was open-mouthed, waiting for Lucy to provide that final, incontrovertible, piece of evidence.

Lucy then sat up straight.

She was going to talk Karen through the evidence.

She asked Karen to cast her mind back to the night before Danny's funeral.

I did not know what she was leading up to. I was unavoidably absent on that occasion.

Karen seemed to focus her mind on recollection. She needed some help and cast a puzzled glance at Lucy, who continued to join the remaining dots.

'Do you remember a strange priest called to see me?'

'Yea', Karen recalled it very well. ' He was the man, who had come home from the missions.

And he had come upon the accident and had comforted Danny'.

'Exactly! He was indeed', Lucy confirmed. 'And do you remember he told me that Danny had asked him to carry the message that he loved me.'

'Of course, I do. It was so poignant'.

Lucy remembered something else, which Karen had seemingly forgotten.

'Think again, Karen, remember the priest said that Danny had mentioned another name to him, which meant nothing to me at the time'.

The wheels were now turning swiftly in Karen's mind.

The two women answered in unison.

'Alfie!'

It was all out now.

My first reaction was for my reputation.

Just as Karen was attempting to dissuade Lucy from confronting Suzi, I felt that same rumbling or churning sensation again.

I was on the move again.


I was back in my hospital ward and just wakening up from a deep sleep.

A doctor was checking my chart.

'Ah, Jack, you are back with us. You had a great long sleep there. How are you feeling now?'

'I feel that I have messed things up for people', I replied with total honesty.

The doctor looked at me closely. He checked my eyes and proceeded to take out a thermometer and take my temperature.

He thought that I was raving.

He seemed reassured.

'You messed nothing up Jack, nothing at all'.

Chapter 50

Karen and I argued the whole way home in the car. I wanted to immediately confront that Suzi woman. Karen was urging me to calm down.

'Think before you act, Karen. Sleep on it and if you still feel like doing it, do it tomorrow'.

It was the advice that I might ordinarily give myself but I did not appreciate it right now. I was raging and not only with Suzi. I wanted to go home. I had urgent business to attend to.

Once back in the house, I went to the storage cupboard in the kitchen and pulled out a roll of black, plastic, refuse sacks. Then, with a puzzled Karen Doyle following me, I marched up to our bedroom and opened the door of Danny's wardrobe. I unceremoniously pulled suits and jackets from their hangers and rammed them into the refuse sacks. Sweaters and shirts filled other bags. All the while, Karen was shouting at me.

'You should not do this in a rush or anger. You will regret this. Mark my words'.

I was in no mood to listen.

'In a rush! You must be joking. Give me a break! These are hanging here for the last year and a quarter. I should have got rid of them long before now. Come on, Karen if you are not going to help me, don't impede me'.

I was growing more and more enraged, as I thought about Danny, having a child by another woman and I crying out for a baby. The bloody hypocrite!

And I virtually, making a shrine of this bloody wardrobe. Wherever he is, he must be laughing at me. It's a good job that he never made it home that evening or I would have killed the lousy bastard.

I released all the pent-up resentment in me over the fact that he left me childless when he knew that I wanted a baby so very much.

Incredibly, Karen was taking on the role of Danny's defender.

'But Danny didn't know, Danny didn't know'. She reminded me.

I was in no mood for rational argument.

'What has that got to do with it?' I roared back.

'If you allow your tomcat out, you can't claim to be surprised when the neighbour tells you that his queen gave birth to kittens. Get real, girl!'

I had the bags packed and they were ready for off.

Karen asked me to leave the bags there until morning and sleep on it.

I was half inclined to let her dispose of them but I feared that she might keep them in her house and present them to me in the morning. So, I flung them into my car, filled the boot with the lot of them as well as having a bag on the back seat.

I then jumped into the driver's seat. Karen jumped in alongside me.

In her rush to dissuade me, she was leaving my house unlocked. She stepped out to close the door. I immediately pulled shut the passenger door of the car before driving off without her.

The charity shop in the car park was always the most convenient for dropping off stuff, without having to carry the bags any distance. I brought in the first two bags. The lady in the shop helped me carry the remaining and thanked me for my donation.

'No, thank you for taking them! They were clogging up my room, not to mention my mind'.

On my return, Karen looked at me with displeasure.

237

I took a bottle of vodka from the drink's cabinet and invited her to join me in a drink.

'Are you going to have me drink this entire bottle on my own or are you going to help me?' I asked.

I left her with very little choice. I pulled out two glasses and a bottle of tonic water.

I filled two glasses and we sat back in the kitchen chairs and took the first of many sips of our drinks.

'I still think that you are being unfair to Danny', Karen said.

'He was with this woman long before he met you. It was not as if he was unfaithful to you or anything like that', she said, attempting to put the matter in perspective.

I was having none of it. In my rage, I considered 'perspective' to be overrated.

'Dress it up as you will but the bottom line was that he had a baby with her and he would not have one with me. What does that tell you?'

She threw her head back in exasperation.

'It tells me that you are being irrational about this. You are only thinking of yourself and not him. Think about how he must have felt driving back into town, wondering how he might break the news to you'.

'Good job for him, that I didn't know it back in February, I would not have bothered hauling his ashes to Dromahair to be scattered. I would have just flung them into the bin with the ashes from the stove.'

'You don't mean that, Lucy. In a day or two, you will see it all more clearly'.

I doubted that very much.

'Karen, have you any idea how difficult it is to think of that Danny and that trollop making a child together?'

'I have no idea but I'm sure it must be incredibly difficult. But that was long before he even knew that you existed. You can't blame him for a past relationship no more than he could blame you for a past relationship or even a future relationship'.

'It's not the same thing', I insisted.

We spoke for another hour, going forward and back over the same points.

One thing I was sure about was that I would confront Suzi and have it out with her.

Then, I thought of something and wondered what Karen's take on it might be.

'A mad thought! I was wondering might it be possible that your Jack, might somehow, have known Danny and wanted to do right by him?'

It would certainly explain a lot.

Karen did not think so.

'Not at all! He never even heard of him until I mentioned him. Why on earth, would you think that?'

'It's just that something about it doesn't quite add up unless there was some familiarity between them. Remember how he tried desperately to keep me away from Peter. It wasn't that he was interested in me for himself but it was like, he felt somehow, looking out for me'.

'True, but by the same token, wasn't he praising Andrew to high heaven?'

Karen had a point there but maybe that was just to frustrate Peter.

'Men can be very devious as you well know', I added.

Karen was reminded of something.

'Oh! Lucy, I have an update for you about the Martin saga. Well, he asked me to go on a Caribbean cruise with him. He said it was to make up for his past sins. And on the subject of trips, Jack asked me to go on a trip around Ireland with him, after he recovers. What do you make of that?' she asked.

I don't think there was much doubt about it. Jack was onto a loser. Martin had certainly raised the bar for poor old Jack.

'I think you should go with Martin on the Caribbean cruise. At least you know that you will be let down by him. Guys like Jack and Danny, while they might appear loyal and trustworthy, actually lull you into a false sense of security and then, they let you down with a bang'.

It was a shocking statement but it was what I felt, then.

'What does all this mean for you and Peter or you and Andrew? She asked.

'Well, I can't say yet but I have made up my mind, that from now on, I am going to do whatever suits me, without consideration for any man. I will do, what most men would do in my situation.

' I will love them and leave them'.

Chapter 51

Karen visited me in the early afternoon.

The hospital can be a dreary place and her visits had become the highlight of my day.

She filled me in on what I already knew but she had surprises for me.

Lucy had discovered that Danny was the father of Alfie. I had to feign shock at the news. Karen was concerned for Lucy. She was not herself at all. She reported that Lucy was like a woman consumed with thoughts of anger and revenge. They way she spoke about her late husband was deplorable.

'I think it is the grief talking', I said by way of reassurance.

'All this reminded her of her great loss'.

Karen seemed to accept this as a plausible explanation.

'Where is Lucy now?' I asked.

'She is with her brother Mark in Sligo'.

'Hopefully, the break will do her some good. Sometimes it's often good to put distance between you and your problems. It gives some perspective'. I figured.

'I hope you are right but I wouldn't bet on it'.

'Maybe those two can talk sense into her, more likely Hazel. Lucy seems to think a lot about her', I speculated.

'Hopefully. Do you know she went and confronted Alfie's mother about the whole thing?'

I did not.

This was major news.

Karen told me that she phoned Suzi, to make an appointment to see her. They met in the hospital car park. From what Lucy told me, it was hot and heavy between them. She accused her of causing Danny's death.

'That was a low blow', Karen reckoned.

The poor mother crumbled and accepted the blame for that'.

She had not thought it all through.

Karen understood that tempers cooled a bit after that expression of remorse and it became a bit more civilised between them.

Lucy had other questions that she wanted to be answered.

I wondered what these could be.

'And did she get any answers?'

'Well, she got some answers anyway'.

Suzi admitted to Lucy that she didn't tell Danny that she was pregnant, because she did not want them to be together, just for the sake of the child.'

Wow! It was all coming out now. I didn't know if I could take any more posthumous assessments of my character. I was not nearly as great a guy, as I had imagined but I don't think that I was quite that bad either.

She also found out how Danny had reacted when she broke the news of the kid to him.

'It hit him, like a bolt from the blue. The poor man did not know what end of him was up', Karen reported.

Lucy also had heard that Danny was more than willing to volunteer his kidney but felt that the whole business would break Lucy's heart. He knew that she would go berserk. Yes, that was my Lucy!

She claimed that from here on, we would be more selfish in her relationships but I could not see that happening. Time would take care of all that.

'No, I think compatibility is the big thing for Lucy'.

Karen pinned me down on what exactly, makes for compatibility.

That was a tough question.

I had to be rather circumspect.

'Well, I suppose, it's the initial spark between people and then it's probably a matter of shared interests or values'.

It was the best that I could come up with on the hoof.

After a moment or so, there came a leading question.

'Do you think that we are compatible, Jack?'

Now, that was a loaded question.

I could not figure, whether it was just idle chat, or whether she had her doubts about where our relationship was going.

Once again, I spoke what I felt in my heart.

'Well, there is little doubt about the physical side of things between us. There is definitely chemistry there. And as for the shared values and interests, I think that we are doing fine. What do you think?'

Karen had her doubts.

'I ask because I have watched Lucy go from a loving wife and a grieving widow to an angry, vengeful woman. That vengeful woman tossed out the last of her husband's clothes after she heard about a previous relationship of his. Now, I am sure she thought that Danny and she were compatible. That makes me wonder whether relationships are just one of life's big lotteries' she sighed.

The news of Lucy throwing out my stuff upset me and threw me for a while. This was something that I had clung onto. It was the last bit of me in her life and I saw her keeping those clothes, as an indication that she had treasured my memory. Now she had tossed them out like she might throw out sour milk from the fridge. It hurt me to the core and saddened me. I did not know what I was thinking or saying and for one unguarded moment, I said exactly what I felt.

'She flung out my clothes!' I blurted out in an angry and accusing tone. 'How could she? '

Karen would have looked on me with less wonder if I had spoken to her in Swahili.

Not your clothes, you fool you! Danny's clothes.'

'Oh of course', I answered attempting as best to recover the situation.

Allowances have to be made for a man recovering from a serious operation.

Karen suddenly became a bit dubious about me.

'Has the doctor been in today yet?' she asked with a note of concern in her voice.

I felt that I had little option but to continue with my dotage.

'I can't remember the doctor being here. Maybe he has'.

She nodded sympathetically.

'Yea, don't stress yourself trying to remember. He will be in soon anyway'.

She smiled and held my hand.

I think I got away with that slip but I could not afford another one.

Chapter 52

The short break in Sligo was just what I needed. I had been highly stressed in recent times.

My childhood home was always a place where I could be myself, and where I was accepted for what I was. I would always be given the time and the space to clear my head. Even over time, nothing had changed in that regard.

I talked at length to Mark and Hazel about Danny's love child. They could understand my confused feelings on the issue but their detachment gave them certain circumspection, which I found to be valuable. Neither of them attached any blame to Danny.

Furthermore, there was no doubt but that he had been so overwhelmed by shock, that he missed the changing traffic light. This made his death all the more tragic.

Each day, I went on long and solitary walks across the dunes in Strandhill and onto the beach. I watched accomplished surfers as they took on the might of the high surf, taking what the sea threw at them and battling on regardless. I sat for hours and watched the tide come in and cover the beach, only for Time to restore the balance gain. Time was already proving to be a friend to me. After miles of walking, sitting, thinking and crying, I came to some understanding of the future I wanted for myself. I was a relatively young woman but time does not stand still. Life is not a dress rehearsal and we get just one crack at it. The end can come very suddenly before we have achieved our goals or sorted out our affairs. I would like to be able to look back on my life and feel that I had done something worthwhile with the years I had been gifted.

I concluded that for me to embrace the future, I needed to consign all of the past to history. That past was over and done with and could not be changed. No amount of bitterness or grief could change that. I would never forget my past but it would never again dominate my present or fashion my future.

Danny was gone. My life with him was gone. That past was gone. The future was all I had now. I needed to embrace that future.

I confess that in my life up to now, I have displayed a huge sense of entitlement and have been guilty of extreme selfishness. I have been blessed with great friends, a lovely house, an interesting job and thankfully I am not short of money.

Danny has seen to that.

I am only in my thirties, with very possibly my best years still ahead of me. Sure, I have been dealt a cruel blow but others, many less advantaged that I, have been similarly hit and have had no choice but to get on with it. I would do the same and attempt to do so, with some grace.

After much consideration and great soul-searching, I had made my decision.

I had chartered a course for my future and I would soon set sail.

Before returning to Dublin, I got Mark to drive me out to Dromahair for one last time to visit the spot where Danny's ashes were scattered.

It was a dry, calm day and the field was empty of cattle. Everything was so peaceful and calm. I remember Danny telling me that he used to come here to gather his thoughts and to consider his future. It was so apt that I should be doing the same now.

I could no longer sense his presence there. It was as if he was moving on too. I decided to speak to him one last time, just in case he was able to hear me.

*'Danny, it's me again. My mother used to say that when your ears are red, it means someone is talking about you. Well, Danny, your ears should have been very red recently. I have learned all about the accident and the child. I know that it must have come as an even bigger shock to you, as it did to me.*
*I haven't got my head fully around it yet but I will get there. I won't be back here again Danny and I suspect that you won't either. Both of us have to move on. It's the way of the world. And when my turn comes to cross over, I hope that you will put in a good word for me.*
*Sleep well Danny and rest in the knowledge that I am OK. Love you forever!*

On my way out of the farmyard, I encountered the young landowner. He greeted me warmly and enquired as to how I was keeping.
'I am doing fine, thank you, but I am moving on and will not be back this way again. So, you take care too and I think that whatever cattle graze in that little field there, they will thrive'.
He nodded rather sombrely.
'Yea, the sun always shines in that field'.
I surprised myself, and him also, by warmly embracing the young man. I remained in the embrace for several moments. I needed that contact.
I bid my farewells and as we drove out the gate onto the roadway, I took one final look backwards.

'Everything all right Lucy? ' Mark asked.
'Yes, Mark. Everything is just fine.

# Chapter 53

Karen drove me home from the hospital but had to return to the office for an important meeting. She promised to call back later in the evening. It felt good to be free of the tubes and the machines. It was also great to escape from the goldfish bowl, which was my hospital ward. I had never got used to being monitored 'round the clock. I felt like a freak. At least now, I might get a break from the constant, undeserved praise. I was embarrassed by my hero status in that hospital. All I could see when I looked in the mirror was the face of fraud.

Now that I was home, I was at a loose end. Others were busy, getting on with their own lives. I would be off my teaching job for many weeks yet. That did not particularly bother me as I was complete fraud there too but at least, it would be a place to go.

On the other hand, it would be a relief not to have to look at Peter's smug face. I hear that Lucy still meets him occasionally, but thankfully, my worst fears have not been confirmed. As for any relationship between her and Andrew, I cannot be certain. Nobody tells me anything ever since I was adjudged to be meddling in her personal life.

Inexplicably, my special powers have been on the wane recently. They had been very active but there has been very little action recently, like a car battery that has suddenly gone flat.

Lucy seems to be unable to forgive me for getting Suzi pregnant but in time, she may become more accepting. I have been trying my best to see events from her position.

Lucy takes a very simplistic view of the matter. In her mind, I had it in my gift to give a woman the gift of life. I gave it to Suzi, but would not give that same gift to her.

The bottom line, as far as she is concerned, is that it is my entire fault. I have little choice but to take it on the chin. There is nothing, I can no nothing to remedy it.

Despite all that I have been through, Lucy is still the only woman I truly loved. I still crave her, as one might crave an addictive drug. I have given away a kidney and don't miss it at all but her absence leaves a gaping hole in my life. She is more part of me than any internal organ. She is in my heart and my soul.

To be with her again, would be Heaven for me.

However, I have to accept that Danny Keane is dead and that Jack Reilly can do precious little for her or indeed for anyone else now.

Karen is a lovely girl, who stood by me, like the loyal and caring person that she is. I have been doing a great deal of thinking lately and I have concluded that I have been doing her a disservice. She deserves better than I can ever offer. I will have to let her down very gently. It will break her tiny little heart but surely that is preferable to her continuing in a relationship with a partner, who is obsessed with another woman.

That would not be fair on anybody.

Over the months, I have grown to like her, respect her and indeed love her but whatever love I feel for her is a pale shadow of the enormous passion, I feel for Lucy. As Cathy said about Heathcliff in *Wuthering Heights*:' I am Heathcliff'.

Well then, on that basis I am Lucy.

I have no choice but to break it to Karen. If it is to be done, then it were better, that it be done quickly. There is no point in postponing it.

Karen will be devastated. I hope Lucy will there for her, as she was for Lucy when I passed away.

Alfie, the only bright note in my life, is mad keen on the trip to Liverpool and it is a trip, which I am looking forward to also. It will be great to see his smile and the wonder in his eyes as he enters the stadium. I imagine that all three of us will give a full-blooded rendition of *'You Will Never Walk Alone'*. The Reds will surely win on that day.

Time was hanging heavily on me. I watched a bit of afternoon television and kept flicking from one useless channel to another.

I began to wonder what people pay their TV licences for. I switched off the television and stretched myself out on the sofa. I placed the threadbare throw around me to keep me warm. I was feeling very tired.

Karen was standing over me when I awoke.

She had a very serious look on her face, like a concerned mother, monitoring a sick child. I roused myself and sat up straight,

She visibly relaxed.

I was not sick just sleeping out of boredom.

She put on the kettle to brew up a pot of tea.

As she made the tea, she shouted to me from the kitchen, seeking reassurance that nothing was amiss with me.

I assured her that I had no temperature and was feeling fine.

'That is a relief. It's great that you can fend for yourself'.

That was probably overstating the matter but I was certainly moving closer to my default state, which was pretty close to being inept.

She returned to the living room and eased herself gently into position, alongside me, as I sat on the sofa. She took a sip of her tea before setting it down on the nearby coffee table.

She began to speak. I felt that she had something meaningful to say.

'Jack, I have been doing a lot of thinking about us especially since you have been in hospital.'

I was afraid that she might embarrass herself by suggesting that we should formalise our relationship.

That would make it very awkward for me to say my piece.

I decided to pre-empt that scenario.

'I was thinking too....',

Karen raised her finger to me.

She had something to say and she was not about to be distracted.

'Please, Jack, don't interrupt me! This is hard enough as it is, without losing my train of thought. I want to say something, which I have been rehearsing for some time and am very nervous about.'

Oh, no! I thought. She is going to ask me to marry her. This is going to be so awkward. I tried to interrupt again but she was having none of it.

'Jack, I have not been entirely honest with you and I am very ashamed of that. Over the last while I have reluctantly concluded that our relationship has run its course'.

What was happening here? That was not in the script at all.

I was dumbfounded.

Karen continued to paint the picture for me.

'I wanted to tell you that but there was never a good time, to say it. Then, you had the operation and I couldn't be so heartless as to break your heart when you were at a low -ebb physically. So I waited until now when you were on the road to recovery'.

I just sat there, open-mouthed and stunned by what I was just hearing.

Karen Doyle was dumping me, not the other way around.

She was giving me my walking papers.

My ego was taking one hell of a trouncing.

It seemed to be one knock after another. I had not foreseen any of this.

How could she?

And she wasn't finished yet. She had more to say.

'Jack, years ago, I went out with this boy, called Martin. When he left me, my heart was broken. I made a brave attempt to move on but I never really managed to get over him. He recently, made contact with me again. He claims that he never got over me either and he wants us to give it another go'.

I nodded sympathetically although I was feeling no sympathy for her.

I had wounds of my own to lick and like a wounded cat, I just wanted to hide away and lick my wounds.

But Karen had more explaining to do.

' I have done a lot of soul-searching and I have concluded that he is the love of my life. I feel that it is fate. I believe that we are destined to be with each other.'

That was all very interesting but I wondered whether this Martin was the sole reason for her breaking up with me.

'If that old flame hadn't contacted you Karen, would you still be breaking up with me today?' I asked,

'I think we would' she instantly, replied.

'I am shocked'. I replied and I was not telling any lies.

'Now, Jack, I know that this is a shock for you and I know that it will cause you much pain in the short term but I had to be honest with you.

I tried not to show my real hurt.

'Karen, you have wrong-footed me on all this. I don't know what to say'.

It will take a while to get my head around it but if your mind is made up, it is made up. There is nothing that I can to change it, especially when Mr Right is waiting in the background'.

That was as gracious as I could manage.

She reached for my hand and clasped it in hers.

'Jack, I'm sorry but I have to be true to myself. It's not you. It's me'.

I was being let down as gently as she could manage it.

Now, I had heard enough and I just wanted her to leave me alone.

But she was not finished.

She had more to say, more salt to rub into my wound.

'Jack, you are such an amazing, generous person and I know that out there, there is some loving and caring woman, waiting for you to come into her life. You will be as happy again and you deserve to be but I am not the woman for you', she insisted.

She released my hand, gave me a quick peck on the cheek, walked out the door and out of my life.

I was on my own again. It was what I had wanted but it was not how I wanted it.

Chapter 54

I announced my plans to Karen. It would be an understatement to say that she was shocked.

'You are going to Ghana! Where the hell is Ghana? She wanted to know.

'It's in West Africa,' I told her.

I let that sink in.

Africa certainly sounded a long way off.

'You are going to darkest Africa. Are you out of your mind?

The notion was anything but mad I figured but I could see why others might feel that way.

She deserved an honest answer from me.

'It has been on my mind ever since Hazel first, spoke to me about it, last February. It seemed so worthwhile. I need a new focus in my life and I think that going to Africa is exactly what the doctor ordered'.

'But you never mentioned anything to me,' she complained, with a hint of disappointment in her tone.

'Well, that was because up until now I didn't have my mind made up. Karen, I have to admit that there was a while when I thought that maybe the two of us might head off but I know that it would have been selfish on my part'.

'I could never be as brave as you Lucy. I am a stick in the mud'.

'You mean that you would never be as mad as I am. Anyway, your circumstances have changed too with Martin and you getting it together again'.

'And I hope that I don't live to regret it', she added.' Anyway, I couldn't survive in Africa with all the strange food and insects, not to mention the hot and sticky conditions. I would miss my home comforts too much,' she admitted.

Twice more, she repeated the word 'Africa' to herself.

'Oh my God, that beggars belief. There am I selfishly, indulging myself on a luxury, Caribbean cruise and you heading off to the wilds of Africa to help the less unfortunate'.

Karen was a great woman to remark on greatly changed landscapes.

'Eighteen months ago, who could have predicted that you would be heading to Africa and I would be back with Martin? Isn't life full of surprises?'

She was not wrong there.

Having heard her reaction, I felt the need to rehearse my reasons, for taking on this adventure. I told her all about my change of mind-set from that of a helpless widow, to that of a reinvigorated, woman, who wants to live a more meaningful life and contribute something to the world.

'Have you told Andrew yet or Peter?'

I had not.

I had wanted Karen to be the first to know.

She deserved that much, considering all she had done for me.

'I will probably tell Andrew tomorrow and I am not that concerned about telling Peter but I will do him that courtesy. It's not as if he is going to be too bothered. There are a lot of eligible women around for him and he is likely to get a lot more from them than he was ever going to get from me. But having said that, I think Andrew will be genuinely disappointed to see me go'.

Karen felt sure that he would.

'Who knows? Maybe he might volunteer to come with you. I hear love stories begin when volunteering overseas'.

I initially dismissed the suggestion but stranger things have happened, if Andrew were to express such an interest, I would have to shoot it down.

I wanted a break, a clean break from my old life, far away from any romantic entanglements or potential attachments. I just want to find myself again'.

What sort of work are you volunteering for over there?'

I filled her in on my plans.

'I will be working with children and especially children with disabilities. They tell me that I will be based in Northern Ghana but I will be inducted in a city called Accra, which I'm told is the capital city. Then I, and a couple of other volunteers, whom I know nothing about, will travel north to work in a place called Tamale'.

Hazel told me, that it would not take long to acclimatise to the place. I intend to give it my best shot'.


Karen shed a few tears. I didn't know whether those tears, were for her, or me but I would guess they were for both of us.

She said that she would be so sad to see her very best friend depart but at the same time, she felt pleased that I had found my mojo again.

'I will miss you so much, Lucy. You were my friend and confidante'.

'Less of the past tense now', I joked, to add levity to a situation, which was in danger of becoming over-emotional for us both.

I assured her that it would not be forever, at the very most, three years.

'I plan to give it two years to start with and if I want to extend that period, I would and if I felt that I wanted to return to Ireland, then I can return at any stage'.

'You are not selling the house so'.

'No, I am planning to rent it'.

She was pleased to hear that.

I tried to cheer her up with the prospect of exciting times ahead for her also.

'You will probably be married to Martin before I come back. Maybe the two of you might honeymoon in West Africa. We can guarantee nice weather and a great tan'.

'Sure thing', she scoffed.

'You line up some fancy hotel and a few Michelin restaurants and we will consider it'.

She enquired about inoculations.

Yes, I would have to get a course of injections before I left and I have to attend a weekend induction course before departure.

'Are you not a bit scared or worried at all? I know that I would be'.

' I might if I had not so much information from Hazel. I feel a bit of excitement. I just want to get out there, get started. I might be helping the natives out there but they might well be, helping me a lot more.'

Karen teased me about coming back with a handsome Ghanaian man.

'Well Lucy, you know what they say: 'You never know your luck.'

I was travelling with an open mind and my attitude will be what is for me won't go past me. I had been eager to have a baby and it became an obsession for me. From now on, I will just let it be, and if it happens, it happens and if it doesn't, then it doesn't.

I feel that I can cope with either scenario.

We continued to speculate on what twists and turns our lives might take over the next few years. Karen was the closest friend that I had or indeed was ever likely to have. I valued her judgment and her honesty. I knew that she would not just tell me what I wanted to hear. There was a straight question, I wanted to ask her and I felt confident that she would give me a direct answer.

'Do you think I'm mad Karen?'

She shook her head with conviction.

'No, I don't think you are mad. I think you are very brave and the more I think about it, the more I feel that you are doing the right thing. I reckon that if you stayed around here, for the next two years, you would either be married to Andrew or still dating Peter and I never thought either of those deserved you. I think that you will find yourself in Africa and I don't think that you will ever regret your decision to go'.

That was all I wanted to hear.

Chapter 55

I was sitting there, still licking my wounds, when I decided that this called for some strong medicine. I was on a skip-load of tablets and I knew it was totally against medical advice but I opened a bottle of whiskey and poured a generous measure for myself.

It didn't seem to do me any harm but it certainly did me no good. I was still hurting. That heave-ho from Karen wounded me deeply. My ego had been badly bruised. I hadn't seen it coming at all. If only I had got in earlier and I would be feeling better now. As it was, I was feeling more and more like a loser.

Lucy was gone.

Karen was gone.

My kidney was gone.

I was feeling very sorry for myself.

Maybe it would take a second helping of whiskey to do the trick.

I poured another glass but I don't remember much about drinking that second one. I must have drifted off into some sort of drunken slumber.

A sharp elbow to my side caused me to suddenly sit up.

As soon as he spoke, I recognised the voice.

Who else but Tommie, my faithful guide?

He was still in the business suit, which he wore when we first arrived in Dublin.

Tommie seemed very angry.

'Will you look at the state of you! Stretched out there on a sofa, stinking of whiskey and wallowing in self-pity'.

I opened my eyes and peered through the alcoholic haze.

'Tommie, why are you here?'

'I'm here to collect you and by the looks of it, I haven't come a minute too early,' he answered.

'What do you mean, collect me?'

'Your time here is over. It's time you got moving again'.

'No, Tommie, I need a little bit more time here'.

Tommie was insistent.

'No, absolutely not! You have done what, you were allowed back to do. The young lad is doing well with the new kidney. And you have done all you can for the good widow, so let's get the show on the road'.

I told him that I had planned to go to Liverpool with Alfie to see a game there.

'Liverpool, my arse! Get a grip, man! You were only allowed back for the benefit of others, not to indulge yourself.'

I felt that I had been a little short-changed.

'Well, it's been no holiday for me'.

'You knew bloody well, that it was going to be tough but that was the price to be paid for being allowed back.

I could feel myself welling up. This, on top of recent setbacks was a bit too much for me.

I started to cry. It was unmanly of course and was not something that I often do but I couldn't help myself.

'Tommie, it's all gone belly-up.

Lucy hates me.

Karen dumped me.

My son still thinks that I abandoned him.

It's an absolute bloody mess'.

Tommie was unimpressed.

'That was the whole point. As I said, returning here wasn't to make you feel good. It was to make others feel better'.

That might well be but I was in no form to accept it.

'Now you listen to me, Danny Keane. You sat with me a year and a half ago moaning and groaning about how your son was in a bad way and how you would do anything to have a chance to help him. You were given that chance. So don't come crying to me now about what Lucy might think or what Karen might think. You knew what you were getting into'.

He was right. That had been the deal.
I tried to salvage something in the way of a consolation prize.
'Is there any chance I could hold on for the Liverpool game or maybe come back again for that game?'
Tommie looked at me as if I had gone soft in the head.
'What the hell, do you think we are running here, Danny? A bloody shuttle service, is it?'
I think that I could take that as being a No.
'Right then, Tommie, so where are we off to now?' I asked.
That's for me to know, and you to find out'
'Am I going up or down? I asked rather anxiously.
'Ah! Things are not as cut and dried as people down here imagine them to be. The Lord moves in mysterious ways'. He added.
It looked like my relationship with Tommie was coming to an end.


I won't be with you after today. My job, as your guide is over once I have you moving again.'
I was less confident now as regards divine judgement and I wondered if he had any insights.
'How do you think I have done, Tommie? Will I be alright?'
'You are asking the wrong man but if it's any comfort to you, I can tell you that there are worse than you around'.
That was some comfort, I suppose!

'What's next for you, Tommie? I asked.

He laughed.

'If I told you that I would have to kill you,' he smiled.

Tommie warned me that I would soon feel a sensation of being transported, much the same as I had experienced in the recent past.

I could cope with that.

'The journey might feel endless but don't panic. It will come to an end and hopefully, you will be grand'.

'Thanks, Tommie'.

'Be good Danny and if you can't be good, be careful'.

Then he was gone.

Soon I felt myself being lulled into a sort of hypnotic trance. There was then, a sensation of being gently, eased into a passageway. I could only describe the sensation, as like being transported on an invisible, conveyor belt. As its speed increased, I found that I was becoming increasingly sleepy.

During the slumber, which followed, I was always conscious of that incessant movement. I was being propelled in a forward direction, whatever that might mean for me.

After what seemed a particularly long time, I felt that I was being transferred into a tunnel of sorts.

In a little while, I sensed that I was not alone but as yet, I could not see nor could I hear anything. I was then conscious of an overwhelming smell of freshness, like one gets from clothes, which had been recently laundered. Was I undergoing a cleansing of sorts?

After what seemed to be an interminable journey of many, many earthly hours, the movement slowed, slowed further and finally stopped. What followed, was a rather strange

sensation of being gently eased down, in the manner of a package on the sloping conveyor belt at an Argos store.
I felt that I was lingering in that state between awakening and sleep.
 The air around me seemed warm, like the air of a Mediterranean sunspot.
Wherever I was, there was a very powerful, sun shining down on me.
I began to hear the hallow voices around me, soft voices, gentle voices.
Initially, they were at some remove, from me but they were coming ever closer to me.
I was startled as if someone had suddenly encroached on my personal space.
Then I heard someone calling out to me.
It was a man's voice.
His tone was one of real concern.
 'Hey, Graham! Can you hear me, Graham?
There was now, more than one voice.
These people seemed to be standing over me.
I felt confused.
I was very slowly wakening from my deep slumber.
I opened my eyes.
I slowly began to focus on those concerned faces, which were now, just inches from my face.
 I realised that I was stretched out on the rock- hard ground.
Two men were standing over me.
They looked concerned.
He nodded to his companion.
'Probably just concussion,' he said. 'He is one lucky man'.
The two gentlemen helped me to my feet.

264

They lifted me and put me on a small wooden bench, in the shade of a nearby tree.

'What happened?' I asked in total confusion.

'You were doing a job on the roof of the school, Graham, when you appeared to stumble. The next second, you fell off. We were worried. Poor George thought you were dead. You were out cold.'

'But where am?' I repeated.

The two men looked at each other in disbelief.

'Can you remember anything at all, Graham?'

I shook my head.

'Relax, you will be absolutely fine in a little while Graham but you need to lie down. You will want to be well rested to welcome the new people, arriving from Accra tomorrow'.

'What people?' I asked, still struggling to make sense of any of this.

'Don't tell me that you have forgotten about the three English men and the young widow from Ireland, who are coming tomorrow'.

I did not know what they were talking about.

'Not to worry! Get some rest. You will be back to your self tomorrow'.

Printed by Amazon Italia Logistica S.r.l.
Torrazza Piemonte (TO), Italy

16392574R00153